Dear Tatum,

Morgan,
   It has been such a pleasure getting to know you via Bookstagram. I absolutely can not wait for the release of All The Yellow Posies! Enjoy!

Cindy Rully xo

Acknowledgments

There are so many people to thank for helping me write this book. Without the encouragement of each of them, *Dear Tatum* would not have made it to the end.

Samantha Lobao, thank you for allowing me to constantly nag and bug you with countless questions on how to make a sentence better. You've read this book in all it's stages and always encouraged me to finish; even during the first, horrible draft I gave you.

Mickey Molar, my wonderful cover artist, you brought these characters to life in a way I could have never imagined. Your determination on making this my dream cover will never be unappreciated. Is there a limit on how many times I can say thank you?

My beta readers, *Adel Mansour*, you're optimism for *Dear Tatum* has pushed me to continue writing. You've made me a better writer through this process and I can't say thank you enough. I am so happy to have met you. *Janelle Mainero*, you're always listening to me complain about how much I hate my own writing and you have no problem telling me to shut up because you believe in me more than I believe in myself. I'm so glad to have you in my corner. *Tory McPartlin*, to know you is a blessing. Your feedback on *Dear Tatum* has made me cry in the best of ways. You've given me continuous support on my writing journey and thank you will never be enough. You are such a light to be known.

Gisbel Ventura, thank you for always hyping up my writing, but making sure to give me the honest feedback I need to make it better. Oh, and I'm sorry for all the times my writing made you cry.

And to my parents, sister and boyfriend, I love you all. Thank you for always supporting me on this journey and believing in me.

authoremilyreilly.com

Dear Tatum

©2019 Emily Reilly. All Rights Reserved. No part of this publication may be reproduced, storied in a retrieval system or transmitted in any form by any means electronic, mechanical, or photocopying, recording or otherwise without the permission of the author.

This is a work of fiction. The characters and events portrayed in this book are fictitious or are used fictitiously. Any similarity to real persons, living or dead, is purely coincidental and not intended by the author.

ISBN-13: 9781696430555

Cover design: Mickey Molar

You may not control all the events that happen to you, but you can decide not to be reduced by them.

―Maya Angelou

Dear Tatum

a novel

EMILY REILLY

ONE
Harper

Love is strange. Love is a journey. Many of us jump on the train to love yet never seem to get there. We crave endless affection and devotion. We yearn for passion so deep we forget about the world around us. That one person becomes our sole world. We want to be able to face them with all our flaws and insecurities and face no judgment in return.

Love deems to be a perfect world and we all desperately want to get there. While at first, we feel weightless, free, and fortunate to have found such a perfect match, it doesn't always end that way. There are times it ends so tragically you never want to return again. Because the truth is, the true colors of a person will always be revealed, whether it treads slowly or hits you all at once. And sometimes it ruins everything you once thought.

The world of love then becomes dim and dark. It reveals it's long claws that creep up your throat and cut you when you least expect it. It haunts your mind and leaves you with scars no one else can see.

This is where I am today. I've been thrown to the side by love's razor-sharp claws, left for the darkness to devour. At forty-seven years old I have no love left to give anyone who crosses my path.

EMILY REILLY

Or so I thought.

I'm standing in a doorway, a doorway that leads to memories I don't want to relive but will never forget. I'm paralyzed by the thought of what can come from this night. If I'm being honest, I don't know why I came. Maybe it's the thought of proving them all wrong.

After all these years, their imaginations still manage to haunt me with the past. The need to prove myself is an urge I've tried to get rid of, but haven't had the confidence to do so. I thought being here standing tall with my shoulders back would convince them I've become secure in my own body. Maybe it would convince them I'm okay with who I am. Part of me is, it's how I was born. But there's another part of me that wishes I was the same as everyone else.

It was never cool to be the outcast, but I was, in my family and in school. I screamed different even with my mouth sewn shut. Maybe it's how I walk or how I style my hair. Maybe it's the clothes I wear.

I've lived for forty-seven years and still at times I feel like being the odd one out can be morbid. I try to convince myself it gives me character—that somehow I can look myself in the mirror and think *I'm unique.* But when everyone around you can boast about things you can't relate too, it can make it that much harder to breathe.

I've learned to navigate life by keeping to myself and holding in my emotions from those who are less likely to understand me. I've discontinued my faith in the church. Those people don't like who I am. But God does, so I talk to Him in places I'm welcomed.

I tried being someone else in this place, but it's harder to pretend when you're sure about who you are. Having a pastor as a father has made being myself more of a challenge. And the thought of him trying to change me has stamped a piece of my life I won't ever get back.

The grip of his hand wraps around my throat. I've never encoun-

Dear Tatum

tered rage such as this. He's restricting my breath. My face is burning, torturing my skin. Black spots blur my vision. And just as I'm about to lose consciousness, he lets go.

I can breathe again. I never valued air more than I do right now. I try to suck in as much as I can. I'm gasping for it. He laughs as he watches, but it's not light-hearted. His eyes are black, just how my vision was moments ago. His hand rises. I brace for what's to come.

My skin is burning even more now. My mother sits and watches, allowing him to hurt me. What kind of mother does that?

"You will never go near her again." His words are slow. "Do you understand me?" His tongue sharpens, harsh like sandpaper rubbing against a chalkboard. My best friend is no longer a friend.

"Harper?" Someone I hardly knew walks in behind me and forces me out of my head. I almost want to thank them. It could've been destructive.

"Hey, how's it going?" I wave as she walks past me. It's time I make my way in. Nausea rises in my stomach, but I ignore it. It's self-inflicted.

My eyes bounce from one body to the other. Familiar faces that look so different surround me. I wonder how different I look to them. Thirty years later and it feels like I'm reliving my first day of high school.

The walls surrounding me carry so many memories, too many for me to remember. Some are faint, some have branded my mind and some are gone, lost, for me to try and find. Secrets, love, and lies have absorbed themselves into this river of thought that flows forever through these very, cracked walls. They've led me to the life I'm living now. And though they're not something I'd want to relive, I credit them for sculpting me.

Everyone is scattering. Their legs run from one body to another. Faces they haven't spoken to since graduation excites them. They feel like kids again, coming back from summer vacation to catch up on everything they've done. I watch. I take it all in, trying not to let my thoughts get the better of me.

My eyes land on two bodies I *really* don't want to see. My heart skips a beat when our eyes meet. An empty soul is staring at me. Chills rummage through my veins destroying all that's in their path. I don't like the look I'm getting. Darkness hovers. I can feel it. I know when it's near because darkness has been a friend of mine for far too long.

Wren turns to me and my name escapes her lips. I shrink in my skin and swallow the lump in my throat. They start to walk over to me. I follow along, but I don't get too close.

Wren and Tatum are nose to nose with me now. She's smiling, but Tatum isn't. He must still be holding onto the past. As they get closer I can see how much they've changed. They look nothing as I imagined. She's not the modelesque woman I thought she'd be. And I'm not one to talk, but I'm surprised time hasn't done her well.

My eyes are drawn to their hands interlocking. Even after all these years, they're still in love. *Must be nice.* But maybe that's why Tatum looks so disheveled. Being stuck with Wren for over thirty years can't be easy.

"You remember Tatum," she says with a perk to her voice. "Obviously." Why obviously? We weren't friends in high school. We were anything but.

I stare at the thin lines withering his face. He looks *so* different. But not in a way that makes him any less attractive. If anything, he's more attractive now with some meat on his bones. I use the term attractive loosely as men aren't really my type.

His stare is dark, almost cryptic. "I could never forget Evan's," he jokes. A smile appears suddenly, catching me off guard. I give him a half, sarcastic smile back and look away.

"The place looks great, Wren," I tell her. "Thanks for the invite." I walk away from whatever disaster was there waiting for me. I neither want nor have the patience to stand there for a second longer.

"Evans?" The voice behind me is familiar, one I haven't heard in way too long. *Brandy Burke.* The one person I can say I missed and mean it.

I can't tell you why Brandy and I ever stopped talking to each other. There was no falling out or a big fight that got between us. We grew in different directions. Looking back, I didn't see it happening. The divide was silent, creeping us apart while applauding itself for achieving an act only the devil would do.

If I had seen our split coming I would've fought to keep it alive and thriving. Brandy was the first friend who allowed me to be me. She never turned her back or got nervous I'd hit on her. And never once did she cower in shame to have someone like me be her friend. It was nice to know there was at least one person out there I could be myself around.

We dive into our lives without missing a single detail—without feeling judged. It's easy to talk to her. She listens and responds, making me feel heard. It makes me wonder how we went all this time without each other.

Talking to Brandy reminds me of how much time I've allowed to slip through my fingers. There are still so many things I want to do, but haven't, either because I don't make the time or am simply just too scared. I can't believe how long it's been since I've lived.

I'm a single mother involved in relationships that never last. I notice the wedding bands branding most people's fingers. They're settled in their lives, living their happily ever after's—at least that's what they want us to think.

None of my dreams have come true. I won't blame it on my past. I blame myself for not letting go of what happened, keeping part of myself hidden from the world—purposely.

Letting another thirty years pass by without the person I'm supposed to be with would be shameful. *I can't let that happen.* I need someone to understand me—*to know me.*

Loneliness always finds a way to weave into my heart. It tortures me with callous words. It scares me. It's something I've never wanted to experience, yet it's all I've ever known. It's one of my many downfalls, an insecurity that's torn down past relationships. But I'm ready to move away from it. I'm ready for my happily ever after.

"I can't believe how different everyone looks," Brandy whispers.

"Speaking of different." I raise an eyebrow. "You'll never believe who came up to me." She shrugs, waiting for my response. "Wren." Her jaw drops. "And Tatum." She's just as shocked as I was.

"I'm surprised you didn't push her up against a wall." I laugh and tell her my fighting days are over. I spare the details. Admitting it was anger that controlled me would mean an explanation for things I can't give an answer to.

But it was mostly Wren I used to fight. She tried to ruin my life. She thrived off of embarrassing me in front of anyone she thought would listen. She had herself on the highest stool she could reach and kept herself there. She was the teacher's pet who married her high school sweetheart, the boy who had it all, the straight-A student, Tatum Barnes. They made me gag.

They still do.

"Evans," Wren walks by me, perking her lips as she shoves me with her shoulder. "You're looking a little extra gay today." I'm not sure what looking gay looks like, but she has an idea in her head and I can't wait to find out what that is. Wren and her friends turn to each other and giggle that horrible, preppy, schoolgirl laugh.

"What did you just say?" Wren turns around and walks over to me. Standing with my shoulders broad, I'm ready for a fight. The fire she's started has been burning for months and it's starting to spread. I'm ready to watch her go up in flames. The people around us are scared of what I'm going to do. They know I don't play nice and they know Wren doesn't back down.

She straightens her back before answering. "It's against the bible to be gay, Evans. I have every right to be disgusted by your choices." Her voice is sharp like it's trying to tear me apart. The fire is burning me now, tearing me to shreds. I can destroy her without using my fists, but today isn't that day.

Dear Tatum

My fingers grip her preppy, collared shirt and whip her against the olive green lockers. Wren clings to her head as she lets out a symphony of tears. I enjoy the sight of her hurt. It enlightens me to know she got at least one thing she deserves.

Without a doubt, Tatum runs to her rescue. He's her knight in shining armor. Her eyes pierce mine as Tatum peels her off of the floor. She whispers words I don't need to hear, "I'll destroy you." I allow her to think and fantasize about what it is she'll try to do next. She knows my strength. I don't hold it down for anybody.

Nobody except him.

Brandy and I have attracted a range of different people who pour into our conversation to join us in emerging into the past. My initial thought of being overwhelmed now feels silly to me. Everything feels *normal*.

I have a beer in my hand, listening to how George puked all over his wife's wedding dress—*on* their wedding day. Needless to say, the reception was almost over, but I guess she never got over it.

We all laugh. The story is actually really funny. But now, I feel kind of funny. I'm overwhelmed and I have no idea why. I'm being pulled away from our conversation. Their words are disappearing, echoing in my head. Circling so fast, I can't piece together the words spilling off their tongues. Pressure is building in my back. I twist myself trying to stretch it out. Just as I turn, a pair of narrow eyes absorb me into their sticky lagoon.

Tatum.

Wren's still glued to his side, taking on another victim to talk to. Their chemistry pours off of them. Their skin never separates. Their hands are gripping body parts deemed private to those who don't know them romantically.

But why is he staring at me? What did I do? He has Wren to deal with. I should be the last thing on his mind. The urge is poking me. I want to ask or wave—*something*. Something to pull me closer to an answer. But instead, I rip myself away.

"You remember Dawn, right?" Brandy asks. She has no idea what just happened. She has no idea the grip Tatum just had on me or the force I needed to use in order to get away.

"Yeah." My voice cracks. "I remember her."

"She's having a get-together in her hotel room. Come with us." I glance at my phone. *10 o'clock p.m.* She knows my kids are grown, so they can't be my excuse to leave early.

"I don't know," I shrug. "I'm usually in bed an hour ago." She laughs, but still tugs on my arm. I'm not sure who else is going and I'm not sure I want to spend another three hours with these people. My comfort time is quickly coming to an end. "I'm going to head home." I give her a hug goodbye. The tears building in her eyes try to talk. An empty feeling crushes me, but I don't give in. I know that's not why she wants to cry.

I swallow the lump in my throat and leave the way I came. I trace my fingers against the olive green lockers. They're *still* the same. I'm *still* the same.

"Evans, wait up!" I turn to see Brandy running towards me. I laugh at how she's running. Her high heels might be a bit too big for a gesture like this, but she doesn't care. And neither do I—as long as she doesn't get hurt. "Please," she says, as she gets closer to me. She's out of breath now. "It's been thirty years, Harper. Thirty." Now it's her voice that cracks. She hasn't called me Harper since the day I met her. It feels weird hearing it come out of her mouth, but it's how I know she really wants me to stay. "If they're still lame, we'll leave." She pops a hand on her hip. She knows I can't say no.

A rush of air shoots out of my nose. "Fine," I say. "Just for a little while." She screeches and levels her fists with her face as she dances. She is exactly who she was thirty years ago.

"You're late!" Dawn yells as we walk into the room. She's chugging a bottle of dark liquor. *Oh boy.* I didn't realize we were partying like we were back in high school, too. Everyone cheers her on as if what she's doing is the most impressive thing they've ever seen.

"We're here. We're here," Brandy says, nodding her head my

Dear Tatum

way. "I had to convince someone to come." I hear the joke in her voice. No one cares enough to comment, but I laugh. It feels nice to be wanted.

"Let's make a toast," Brandy suggests.

Dawn shakes her head. "We have to wait for Tatum. He should be here any minute." *What?*

The door opens from behind us and Tatum makes his way in. I gulp. My hands are shaking enough for me to feel self-conscious. I wait for Wren to appear, but she never shows.

He smiles as he walks in, making eye contact with everyone but me. I'm surprised by his sudden change in behavior. How downstairs his eyes wouldn't look away from me, yet now, they won't even come near me. There's something different about him. He seems more enigmatic these days.

Brandy's voice protrudes the air forcing me out of the daze I've set myself in. "To the class of '85. To life, to meeting again and to new beginnings." *New beginnings*. I hope that's true for me, too.

I bring my glass to my lips and gulp down the much-needed shot, and then watch, as everyone's face turns sour. We all laugh at how hard it was to take. It's not as easy as it used to be, but it was fun. *I'm having fun.*

There's little to no tension now, thankfully. With almost everyone here gone off of the one too many shots they've taken, it makes it easier to have a conversation. Most of it is nonsense. But we all seem to care a little too much. It could be the booze. It's definitely the booze.

Tatum's eyes must have found someone else to grip. And I'm relieved to say the least. He looked like a monster downstairs. Dangerous and fatal. But I begin to question myself. What would make him switch up so fast? Or was it me that was delusional? Maybe it was my own unveiled mind that decided to concoct a story that wasn't true. Why? To make me feel special? It's easy to do when you've been damaged so many times.

There's no reason for Tatum to want me. We weren't friends in high school. I can't even say we were acquaintances. His high school sweetheart *hated* me. I wonder where she is now. Banging another dude behind his back? She has the will to try at least. I would know.

"Please tell me I'm not the only one who noticed Tatum grilling you downstairs." I jerk my head towards the voice whispering in my ear. Brandy keeps a smile as she digs into the cloak he's hiding under. "He so wants you," she smirks.

I sigh and roll my eyes. "Not at all. And even if he did, I'm not interested in a married man," I say. "Especially not Wren's husband."

Her eyes widen with panic. "I didn't know you didn't know." I have no idea what she's talking about. "They broke up right after high school. Haven't been together since," she says, taking a swig of her drink.

"Then they miss each other. Did you not see how they were acting downstairs? I never would've been able to guess they broke up with how far Wren was lodged up his ass." She laughs. I don't. My brows knit together and my gaze falls back to Tatum. *What does he want from me?*

Everyone's falling asleep and there's no way I can drive home. After three shots and about six beers, I'd be more likely to end up in jail than my own bed. Brandy and Dawn are sprawled across one of the two beds. The rest of them crawl into whatever crevice they can find. I assume Tatum's somewhere mixed in, but I pray he left. I'd hate to come face to face with him again. Actually, I might die if I do.

I sit in the chair and force my eyes shut. I move my shoulders around, but the designer of this chair made it clear that nobody, and I mean nobody, sleeps in this chair.

The air is stuffy and I no longer have the desire to sleep. Between drinking and the room being too crowded for comfort, I need to step outside before I suffocate.

I step onto the balcony and when I'm finally alone, with the door shut, silence takes its turn. It screams into my ears. It's so loud it almost physically hurts my being. I'm forced back into my own head, thinking about what the next thirty years will look like. All I can see is black. Nothing comes to mind. I'm not surprised. I've done nothing to support my future. I've come to terms with letting myself down.

"Can I join you?" I look up and Tatum's stepping onto the balcony. My mind floods with Brandy's words. *He so wants you.* My heart starts to pick up pace, along with the steadiness of my hands. This is it. My final moment is having to look at Tatum's face one last time. Tell my kids I love them.

Everything goes black.

I pinch my eyes open a tiny bit. I'm alive and Tatum's still next to me. I don't know what to say, but we're sinking in this river of stillness that's getting too hard to stomach. "I thought you were sleeping," I say.

"Just resting my eyes." I don't know what to say, so I don't say anything. I'm not sure what he's expecting from this, if anything at all. Is he out here because of me or was he too suffocating in there? I don't want to ask.

"So," he draws out the 'o' as if he has something on his mind. "Thirty years, huh?"

I nod my head. "Yup."

"Crazy."

"Very." Our words are short, and his intentions remain unclear. I can't tell if I'm going crazy or if he really is giving off a feeling I can't read. I continue to stare out into the space in front of us, and we sit in a silence that teeters from awkward to comfortable.

"You married?" He asks.

I brace myself. "No," I say. He's silent. His head falls backs and a loud sigh shoots out of his mouth. I slide my stare over to him, confused. "Are you—are you mad?"

"No," He throws his head down just enough for the light to hit *his* angle. He laughs, neither quietly nor loudly. It's gentle. "Not at all."

"You know I'm gay, right?" I break my own rule and make eye contact. His top teeth graze his bottom lip. "Right?"

He nods. "No kids then?"

God, this conversation is painful. "I have a 24-year-old and my youngest is 19. You?"

"Two." His eyes meet mine again. They flicker a dark light that burns the surface of my skin. "Did you adopt?" He asks.

"Impressive," I say, laughing to myself. His face scrunches. "Not many people have the courage to ask such a blunt question." He shrugs. "But no, they're not. I was married to a man a long time ago."

"I thought—"

"I am," I say, rolling my eyes. "I'd consider it more of a sacrifice than anything else. It was something to make my father happy." It feels good saying that out loud. It wasn't something I hid, but not something I ever announced. We weren't a love story. He wasn't the one man to sweep me off my feet and change who I am. We weren't a fairytale. But he gave me my children, and for that, I wouldn't change a thing.

"Now I'm impressed," he says.

"With what? The fact that I tried to change who I am in order to have a father that loves me?"

"It's heroic." He straightens his back and stretches his arms up. He moves effortlessly. I watch as his mouth widens to the beat of his yawn. The darkness in him is fading. Or maybe it was my own despair hovering him. *Maybe.*

I catch him staring at me. Teeth to lip. Eyes low. Breath steady. There's something changing in him.

"My father left me when I was a kid," he admits. "I could never please him either." His eyes fleet from mine, hiding the layers of truth he keeps hidden. "Tried to change who I was for him, but damn," he says. "It was never enough." Sacrificing your life for someone else is one of the most painful things you can put yourself through. "I thought that if somehow I could be someone else he'd love our family a little more. But it didn't matter who I was." He shrugs it off as if it wasn't the hardest thing he's had to deal with.

Our similar wound surprises me. He's always portrayed a perfect life, but the way his eyes dim, it's obvious he still hurts.

His confession has merely opened up the wound I thought I sewed up years ago.

Warmth covers my hand. I look down to see his fingers grazing mine. We share a moment of both comfort and displeasure. Two damaged souls so far apart somehow come together to help one another. We've been distracted by these thoughts all our lives.

Our stare finds each other. Hope seeps from our pores. It's our pain that connects. An urge surfaces in my stomach. It's an act I don't want to pursue. I don't, but *he* does.

He leans in, lips first. Pulling away doesn't cross my mind, but neither does kissing him back. An usher of panic is rising. I'm shaking. I'm nervous. I'm scared. I don't know what to do. *I freeze.*

He pulls away, shame lingers on his face. "I'm—I'm so sorry," he shakes his head. I feel oddly connected to him right now. I'm not sure if it's the alcohol or the wound we share.

I surprise myself by pulling him back. Each hand has a fist full of his shirt. My name slips out of his mouth in a whisper. Before I can say anything back, he pulls me in deeper. He's confident enough to slip his tongue in my mouth. I reciprocate.

Our tongues dance for a while, but that doesn't mean I like it. I don't know if I do. I don't know if I'm supposed to. His kiss is rough, rougher than any woman I've been with. It's hard to tell if it's his gender or if it's him. I haven't had enough experience to tell.

We both lean back at the same time. Separating our lips feels like a chore, but this kiss can't last forever. "So." Now I'm the one dragging the 'o'. "That was—"

"Out of the blue? Random? A surprise?"

"All of the above." I tilt my head downward and laugh softly. He laughs with me. Neither one of us understands what just happened. My hand covers my mouth, but not for any particular reason. Just a reflex of embarrassment.

The knot in my stomach is growing at unseen speeds. Why did that feel so right? *He so wants you. He so wants you. He so wants you*. I would hate to hear what Brandy would have to say about this.

I convince myself this was a spur of the moment kind of thing. I tell myself his lips are not the ones I'm meant to kiss forever.

This is a one-time thing.

One time.

That's it.

"Do you still live around here?" The words come out boxy as if I'm stuck in a talking electronic. Moving us into another subject will be good for both of us.

"Southern California." *Perfect.* "Two houses in Malibu." *Rich.*

His accomplishments have paid off. He owns two houses and I live with my mother. Let that sink in. And even though I only moved back in to help care for her, I still have to say I live with my mom. It's not the most attractive thing to say when trying to impress someone. *Not that I'm trying to impress him.*

"Warm weather all year round?" I smirk. "You're spoiled." It's nothing like living here in Leavenworth. Cold. Damp. Dark. Just like most of the people who reside here. They fit like a puzzle. I'm actually jealous of the weather where he lives. It's been a lifetime dream of mine to leave this town and live down south.

"I'd much rather be up here," he says. "I love the cold."

"Are you human?" We laugh, *again*.

His eyes search the parking lot looking for something he won't find there. Somewhere deep inside of him is a question he's longed to know the answer too. It's stamped onto his face, but I don't have the courage to ask what it is.

"I don't know many people who endure cold weather for enjoyment," I say.

"Well my wife—" *Wife?* "She was born in Southern California and wanted to raise our kids there." I press my lips together. Looking away, my cheeks flush with shame. I can't believe I fell for his trick. "That's not what I meant," he says. His hand finds the top of my knee. It sits there, but only for a moment. "We've since got a divorce."

"Ah," I say, glancing down at his hand. No ring, but that doesn't mean it's not hiding somewhere in his bags. "The old divorce tactic."

"Really," he explains. I can see the distress on his face. "I separated from that a long time ago." *That?*

"Oh, I'm sorry." I'm trying to believe him. I don't have any reason not to.

"Don't be," he says. "It was needed. The marriage was doomed from the start. She isn't the best kind of person to surround yourself with. I'll just say that." He looks away and off the balcony again. I wonder what he's thinking. I wonder what he thinks of me.

"I've had a few of those in my lifetime." He looks over at me. He has the same look on his face as he did right before he kissed me. But I don't want him to kiss me again. I'm not ready for that.

We chat for a while longer. Things like life and love are the topic of conversation. Tatum has lost a part of himself because of his father and his disappointing marriage. Both of those things are tough to swallow.

Pain is no easy task to get over. It takes time and patience to heal. I think it's easy to say we're both still healing from our past. Tatum loves hard, it's easy to see. He likes to be liked. He likes to feel loved. I do too.

In high school, we had no similarities, or so we thought. But sitting here tonight, I've realized our lives are a lot more similar than we thought. It makes me think of how many people I've judged, yet never even knew.

I don't know what any of this means, but I feel okay, content with what tonight has brought me. Somehow, it's helped bring me back to life.

TWO
Sadie

Marriage is strange. Before we have it we dream endlessly of its simplistic beauty. You love a person and that's it. Having a ring on your finger is your happily ever after. But isn't marriage more than *just a ring*? It's more than *just love*.

Marriage is a ride that carries you on countless roads. It'll make you mad, crazy, maybe even delusional. But there's magic in it. It has the power to mend two souls together. That's impressive.

I'll say most of us crave the feeling of a bottomless love. Perhaps it's the feeling of being the luckiest person on earth. But what most fail to see is that marriage has a dark side to it. It's the side everyone keeps quiet. It's the side that will work tirelessly to weed you apart. The side you need to fight through.

I assume most couples are still going through the honeymoon phase when they get married. But what happens when that feeling stops? When it's been ten years, you have three kids and neither you nor your spouse are the twenty-pound less beings you once fell in love with? *What then?*

But feeling like you've fallen out of love doesn't mean you

Dear Tatum

actually have. I believe it's normal for most couples to go through distant phases.

There's a reason you announced your vows to the entire audience of your wedding. There's a reason you showed your most vulnerable side to the people you don't confide in. Love makes you do things you normally wouldn't.

Love is crazy.

And when things go wrong, love hides. It hides in the anger outbursts, the jealous stares, even the little pit of grudge you've had burning at your core for the last twenty years. Sometimes those reasons build up so high you can't see the other side anymore.

Your view is obstructed by mounds of brick. The easy thing to do would be to walk away—leave for a clearer path. But if you skip the easy route and dig to the root, you'll find something much more promising. Each brick is placed on individually, which can only mean just one can be torn down at a time. That thought alone may make anyone go insane. It'll feel like love no longer wants you in its realm. But that's hardly ever the case.

It's not easy by any means. Sometimes things happen that seem unforgivable. People lie and say things they don't mean. People become untrustworthy, making it even more difficult to want to move forward. So, patience is going to be needed. In fact, a lot of it will be needed in order to tear down that wall.

And if I'm being honest, this is where my marriage stands right now. A place where hardship, pain, and ache rest themselves on me daily. It's been scaling our marriage for a while, but I married my husband for a reason. And I have to remind myself of those reasons every morning before the feeling of giving up sets in. We know the truth of each other's hearts.

Or so I hope.

I roll over and the empty feeling in my stomach mimics the empty spot in our bed. It's been three days without Tatum. It's harder than I thought it'd be. It stung when he told me he was leaving. "I could've found a babysitter for us," I told him. But it was too late. He waited too long.

We've been on the verge of destruction lately. Simple things like who'll pick the kids up from school or who supposed to shut the light off before bed has cradled us into a dark space.

I've been trying to look at this weekend as much needed time apart. We've been so on top of each other the past couple of months. This time away can be restorative, as individuals and as a couple. *I hope.*

He left with no word, no warning. I woke up and he was gone. *It was painless.* I didn't hug him good-bye. I didn't get to lay my lips on his. I didn't have a chance to work myself up. I didn't miss the goodbye, but it sure made me miss him. Absence can really make you miss a person. Even the person you wish you could take a break from.

The airport doors in front of my car taunt me with images of Tatum. My heart quickens every time I think it's him. Minutes don't want to pass. They're dragging their feet.

Another body emerges from the doors. I don't get my hopes up. I assume it's another businessman coming out to his limo. But he gets closer. And closer. *And closer.* My heart's now drumming on the inside of my chest with pleasure.

There he is. I lean in and cradle him, hoping for a rush of enchantment. His arms are tight around me. I lose balance and fall into the car. We share a moment of quiet laughter. His hug makes me feel like I'm his again.

Very few words are spoken during our ride back home. Both my hands rest firmly on the steering wheel while his thumbs dance on the keyboard of his phone. This isn't how I expected our first moment back together, but I'm not disappointed.

A smile cracks the sides of my lips. I'm eager to hear

about his trip. I want to hear stories of him running the streets with his childhood best friends. I want to hear that he went to an old bar and got hammered for no reason, or even him sitting with an old friend talking about the last thirty years. *Anything.* I just want to hear his voice.

"How was it?" I squirm in my seat waiting for the stories to start, waiting to hear about how everyone looks and acts so different. Or maybe exactly the same.

"Good." The word slides out with a sigh. His phone consumes him. His thumbs are *still* dancing. They're *still* creating words I can't see.

Still.

The urge to know who it is grows, but I'm hesitant. Too many questions annoy him. An un-happy Tatum is not someone you want to be around. "Were people happy to see you?" I ask, treading lightly.

"Yup," he says. I jerk my head just enough for him to notice. He looks over and his stare pinches me. I don't care if unhappy Tatum comes out. At this point, he's just being a jerk.

"Who is that?"

"It's work, Sadie." He mumbles harsh nothings under his breath. I guess his hug wasn't as promising as I hoped.

"They could've called me," I say. "What the hell is an office manager supposed to do if no one treats them like one?" Heat seeps from even his smallest pores. He's brewing now. I'm waiting for his words to rip me apart, but he says nothing.

Nothing.

"Are you going to answer me?" I ask.

"You know I've been trying to give you a break." I hate being handled like I'm fragile, like somehow I turned into a flower and the slightest blunder will crinkle my insides and damage me for life.

"I'm fine to work, Tatum." I keep my lip short and tight, trying to convince myself along the way. He has a bad habit of treating me like a child sometimes. His caring essence can come off controlling, sometimes even pretentious. But I'm a woman who can fend for herself. I make the right choices. I know what I need and what I don't need. And unfortunately, my husband has a hard time recognizing that.

I sort between the couch cushions to lay my hands on the vibration. "Come on," I mumble under my breath. I stretch my hand as far as it'll go. Finally, I reach it. Dad's nursing home. *"Hello?" Their voice is low, subdued.* Fuck. *The phone falls from my hand. This can't be real.*

Tatum walks in. His skin falls blanched, almost sickly. "Baby," he cries. "I'm so sorry." He wraps his arms around me and nestles me into his chest. "You can cry. It's okay. I know you want to cry." Part of me doesn't, but another part does. "It's okay to cry," he says again. Misery hits and reality sets in.

It's been an adjustment not having him around. It's not easy admitting life hasn't been the same. I should've been somewhat prepared for his death but I wasn't. Not at all.

Growing up with a careless mother was always hard to navigate. She was selfish and cared only for herself. Yet, my father somehow managed to make up for it. He went far beyond what any mother should do. Neither one of us knew how this worked, but we made it. We grew together as father and daughter and then, best friends. So not having him around has been strange. Very, *very* strange.

But then again, death is so incredibly strange. Our body finds even the smallest of reasons to ache. Remembrance harbors and pain undoubtedly follows. We crave the touch of their skin so bad it frays the deepest parts of our bones. Tears fall and brand our skin with memories that hurt. Everything we once lived seems like a dream.

It's strange that suddenly we no longer have that life around us. No longer do you have them to confide in, or to hug, or to even look at and feel their presence. They've been ripped away like they weren't an attached part of our being.

But if you're even the slightest bit spiritual, you'll know their soul is somewhere at ease, at complete peace. That thought alone should bring us comfort because it's no longer about us, but about them and the well being of their soul.

We tend to these tragedies with our own selfish emotions. Our loved one knows the mystery no one here will ever understand. Everlasting life. Happiness beyond what our physical bodies can endure. *The beyond.*

We know everyone has their time. We know our closest loved ones—even ourselves—last moment can be now. But the truth is, we're never prepared. Death can spring on us with no warning. It's shocking, absolutely devastating. Our world will be crushed and bruised. Our tears will still fall. They'll still hurt. But we must stay strong for those we lose. Not for ourselves, but for them. We must continue to live, if not for ourselves, but for them.

I must live if not for myself, for my dad, for my children, and for my marriage. He would want that. I should want that. My heart may be burning, it may feel like fire is the only thing consuming me, but I have to live.

I can live despite a shaken world.

THREE
Sadie

Tatum's been home for five days. His thumbs are *still* dancing. Questions circulate my mind, ones that haunted me earlier in our marriage. I no longer think it's work consuming him.

Snooping through his phone is something I've learned not to do. But saying it doesn't cross my mind would be a lie. I'm desperate for the truth and Tatum's words feel empty. But going through his phone can destroy a lot of things we've worked towards.

Tatum gives me space, sometimes too much. But I'm trusted, that's the point. He counts on my loyalty and never questions it. He doesn't blink twice to any of the words I have to say. Sometimes that hurts. No one is perfect.

Everyone has demons.

I monitor his behaviors. They're similar to the past hurt he caused our family, but I haven't made any sudden movements. I don't want the extreme to surface. Not yet. I'm putting my trust in him. Time will share what I need to know.

"What do you want for dinner tonight?" I ask.

"I'm going out tonight, babe." My eyes narrow. "I'm taking everyone at work out for dinner."

Dear Tatum

"I'm not invited?"

"Didn't think we had a sitter." I devour the screams climbing my throat. His face distorts into something that makes me sick. Walking away, I drag my feet waiting for him to pull me back, to promise this wasn't a deceitful move. But he doesn't. He allows me to tread away slowly, shamefully.

He's home. Hair messy and tie out of place. He thinks I'm sleeping, but the strain of his absence has led my body into a constant burning pain. "Looks like you had fun."

He stiffens when my tension hits him. He rolls his eyes. He strips down to his boxers and gets into bed. "Good night," he says, turning his back towards me. The lingering scandal sleeps on his skin. I can smell it.

I roll on my side only to be battered with the LED light making a scene on the ceiling. I can hear his thumbs dance. Tiny slits carve the inside of my heart but don't quite make it to the surface. Not yet at least.

Picturing the things he may be saying to the face hidden behind the screen makes me queasy. I wonder if he plays a different man than who he really is. The urge to rip his phone from his hands grows inside of me, weaving tenderly through my veins.

I want to *scream*.

I want to *rip* the house apart.

A burning ache *tortures* me.

Silence prevails. Snores start seeping from his cracked lips. Now would be the only time to make a move—to slip away and find the truth.

Tiptoeing around the bed I try not to make even the faintest of sounds. Cradling his phone in my hands, I slip out of the room and down the stairs.

I take a seat at my kitchen table and prepare for my life to flip. *Again.* My fingers wrap around his phone waiting to unlock the secrets hidden inside. I almost change my mind. I almost don't want to know. I don't want to feel what I once had to feel.

Confronting emotions is hard for me. Healing is even worse. Is now even a good time to re-open a healing wound? I'm not sure what I'll do with the information I see anyway. Is it worth ripping myself apart? I know I'll forgive him. It's what I do best. It's the only thing I can do. It's what my guilt *makes* me do.

I breathe for a moment to calm my nerves, or I try to at least. I'm not sure if it works.

Breathe in.
    Breathe out.
Breathe in.
    Breathe out.

I copied my fingerprint in Tatum's phone months ago incase I was in a situation like this again. I thought if I ever needed it I would press my thumb to that button and dive into the world he was living behind my back. I thought I'd tear him apart with words so harsh he'd be on his hands and knees begging for my forgiveness. But that time feels like it's now. And right now, I don't think I want to do that.

I can hear the clock ticking. Time is not on my side. It's now or never. My thumb finally presses down the home button and I start to scroll, hesitantly. My stomach plummets when I press the message icon, afraid of what's going to be waiting for me.

Nothing shows. No mystery woman. No, *I love you* texts. No naked pictures. Not even a message from any of his colleagues. Nothing except messages from me.

You'd think not finding any explicit content would mend the frail cracks braiding my heart, but it doesn't. The uneasy feeling squeezing my stomach is still here. But now it's stronger. There is power in the delete button. In a matter of seconds, all evidence is destroyed. The delete button gives him power. A lot of it.

I know I'm not the only one who texts him. What about

his mom? Alisa? The rest of the people from work?

I want to wake him, ask him who the hell is taking all of his attention away. What's the sudden interest? But I don't. I already know what I'll get.

What are you talking about?
Are you that insecure?
Will you ever let the past go?

I place his phone back where he left it. I'm not angry, but I'm not happy. I'm—*blah*. Tatum's facing me now. I stare at the lines on his face. Years worth of stress covers him. They're shallow but noticeable. I wonder what each one represents. I wonder if each line is a lie he told. I wonder what my lines mean.

I'm jealous he can sleep through pain such as this. I'm jealous he's able to make mistakes that can break his family without hesitation.

My restless legs dance with the secrets hiding in between our sheets. I'm exhausted, but I can't stay still. I need to be somewhere else, somewhere my mind can forget about Tatum and the cipher he's created. My dreams will do me no good. They have a bad habit of dragging me to the worst places.

Not caring if it wakes him up, I turn on the lamp next to my bed. I want to read. I need to read. I grab the book that's already next to me. It's a scary world, but it's better than the one I'm living in right now.

Tatum's eyes peek open, checking his phone before anything else. I'm not sure if it's to check for messages or to see the time. I don't care enough to ask, though I probably should.

"Can't sleep?" He asks, eyes still half-closed.

"Nope," I bark back keeping my eyes still on the words in front of me. He adjusts himself upwards, sitting identical to me.

"What's wrong?" He attempts to take the book from my hand, but my grip is faster than his.

His eyebrows arch in a way that tries to make him appear innocent, but it's not working. The way his face wrinkles, as he tries once more to adjust to the light, rubs me the wrong way. This is a dangerous game he's playing. I'm losing patience. I'm losing what I need to make this better. The words I don't want to say are spilling.

Who's on the phone?
Why are you so preoccupied?
Who is taking you away from our family?

He leans back. His eyes have fallen to his lap. He tucks his chin into his neck. The cracks in my heart are expanding. He's silently admitting my fears are true.

But the words that escape his mouth don't line up with his reaction. "I don't know what you're talking about." My jaw clenches and my fists tighten into a ball.

"Do you expect me to believe that?" My voice drops and my lungs free the darkest part of my wrath. "Your face has been stuck in that phone since you've got home from your reunion. I notice it, the kids have noticed it, we've all noticed, Tatum. So who is it?"

His hands grab mine and despite how angry I am, I don't pull away. "There's no woman on that phone. There's no sex happening behind your back. There's none of that," he says. "You are my wife. I want to protect you. I want to take care of you. I want you to be happy, Sadie. Your father's death has taken a toll on you whether you like it or not. You need time to heal. You need to take a step back and breathe. You dive into things and let them consume you without taking the time you need. And if you aren't going to do it, then I'll do it for you." I listen to every word his lips form. "I've told everyone from the office not to contact you. I know you don't want to hear it, but you need time. I can see how it looks like I'm snooping around behind your back, but that's the last thing I'd do to you. We aren't falling backwards, Sadie. I promise."

We aren't falling backwards.
I promise.

FOUR
Sadie

Two naked bodies lay together as one. Tatum's skin brushes against mine and I can feel the trail of where he's been line my body. His fingers dance with my hair as our tongues circle around each other's mouths. Our bodies' tangled and hot, drip old love for the bed to taste—for us to remember after this moment is over.

Butterflies dance around my stomach, leaving me with a feeling I've missed. It's been so long since I've felt his touch, I hadn't realized how much I've craved it. But this helped the light peak through. And maybe, just maybe, we'll be okay.

The feeling in the pit of my stomach is similar to the day we first made love. It builds hope and encourages me to continue fighting for our marriage. "I love you," I say, nibbling the bottom of his ear.

I quiet my breath and wait for him to tell me, "I love you, too." But his lips graze my neck instead and nibble along my collarbone. I lean back to look at him. His eyes meet mine and I search for the three words I need to hear.

But I can't find them.

I can't find anything.

"I love you, Tatum." My voice breaks.

"Me too." A quick gasp fills me. Two words. All it took was two words to destroy this moment. I wasn't looking for a, *me too*. I want an, *I love you*.

He fails to read what's written all over my face. He leans in to kiss me again, to pick up where we left off, but I can't bring myself to that space again. "Tatum." His name spills off my tongue in a whisper. I push him away and he leans back, tucking his chin into his neck. "I just told you I loved you." The need to cry lingers in the corners of my eyes, blurring my vision. But I won't weaken my strength in front of him. He'll get the wrong impression. "Do you still love me?" It hurts just to ask.

"What kind of question is that?" His voice sharpens as if I'm in the wrong.

"Then say it," I say. He sits quiet and it feels as if time has stopped, as if the sun will never rise again and we'll be sitting in this warped world forever.

Waiting for the truth takes forever. His eyes are hollow, waiting to encase me in tragedy. If he admits his love is gone, this will be the end of us. Possibly the end of me. "I love you, Sadie," he finally says, but his words hold no hope. No promise. *No love*.

It's hard to think just moments before I was high on our re-kindling love. Now I'm slouched over on the bed questioning everything. But I guess this is a part of healing. I need to keep telling myself this. I need to know there's an end to this mad world we're circling.

I scurry past him and put my clothes back on. Coffee's what calms me and right now, I need a lot of it. A piece of me breaks when he decides not to run after me.

I can't bear to think about another pair of arms holding me like I'm theirs. It's confusing but I need to make this work. There's an obsessive need to stay with him, for reasons I can't confess.

There's only one person I know who can calm this thunder. She can usually see what I can't and right now, I need her to tell me I'm going crazy. I need her to tell me the hesitation in Ta-

Dear Tatum

tum's voice was merely a funnel of destruction made up by me.

"Sadie?" I recognize the voice coming from behind me, but it's not who I'm meeting. I adjust in my seat to look back. *There is no way.*

"August?" My mouth hangs open and my stomach twists into a knot I don't think I can untangle. "What are you doing here?" I ask, remembering his full hatred for coffee. He went as far as making sure not even a single coffee bean entered his house. The smell alone made him gag. It always used to make me laugh.

"I have to admit," he laughs. "Coffee is kind of my thing now." His eyes bounce off the seat in front of him, soon meeting mine. He wants to sit but isn't going to say it.

Staring into the face of a man whom I haven't seen in ten years feels eerie. He's identical to what I remember. Short hair with a swoosh of gel, eyes that are stern, yet have a way of comforting you, lips that are just the right size, and a jawline that isn't nearly as sharp a bodybuilder, but sharp enough to realize he loves the gym.

"How are you?" We laugh quietly realizing our lips formed the same words at the same time. I don't understand why he's so happy to see me when we left on such bad terms. Lips that should be frowning in complete rage are actually smiling.

"I'm good," he says. Our eyes float away from each other and all that fills us is the sound of coffee being brewed.

The void building between us makes him uncomfortable, so he starts to fill it by catching me up on the last ten years of his life. His lips hold my gaze. Watching him maneuver the words he lets out sends me into a trance I can't find my way out of. I always pictured an icy chill accompanying us when we met again, not this kind of contentment that's filling me.

I listen carefully to the tone of his voice more than the words coming out. He's gentle, kind, and nothing as I expected he'd be. "How are you?" He asks again. He tilts his head as if he's waiting for me to reveal what karma has done to me. But I don't know how to answer. I actually wish he never asked. The last thing I want to do is admit that I'm nothing more than okay, especially not to the man who once held my hand.

I can picture it now. Laughter, tears of joy, and thrill just seeping out of his pores, excited I finally got everything I deserved. So instead, I nod. "I'm fine." I can feel his eyes scanning every inch of me. Part of me wishes I never paid my favorite coffee joint a visit. Another part of me loves that I did. A part of me wishes Wiley would walk up right now. While another part of me wishes she never does.

August bites his lip, though not meaning it to be in any way sexual. But my eyes narrow to that bite and my thoughts stampede the logical part of my brain. I look away, afraid of any more thoughts contaminating my mind.

"August," I say his name without knowing what's coming next. "I'm sorry." I close my eyes and wait for his words to dress me with pain. But when I look up, his eyes are wide, smiling at me.

Forgiveness can be hard to accomplish, especially when the damage is devastating. But somehow, August is stuffed with forgiveness. It's puzzling. I don't know how anyone can forgive a person who's destroyed their life and their future, forcing them to build from the ground up.

August is screaming. His voice is raspy. It's losing its sound. I've never encountered rage such as this. But when the one person you trusted most betrays you, anger seeps in easily. "You slept with one of my employees, Sadie! What the hell is wrong with you?" I stand there facing towards him, ashamed of this harsh reality. My shoulders slump forward trying to push away the truth that's baring knives right into my chest.

I'm numb. I hurt the only person to ever love me. But I don't regret what I did. It had to be done. "I'm sor—"

"No, you're not!" He screams. "You never would've done this if you were sorry." Fire is burning behind his eyes, while the smoke

Dear Tatum

escapes his lips.

"August, I'm sorry you're hurt." I swallow the knot that's crowding my throat. "And I'm sorry for what I did, but I love Tatum. And I know I should've broken things off with you before we got physical, but I didn't and I can't change that." He runs his hands through his hair and looks down.

"So what now?" He asks. "You're leaving me?" His eyes dodge mine, staring at anything that's not me. "You're going to leave me for a fool who doesn't have a job anymore?" His eyes are swollen with a wall of tears waiting to escape his burning heart.

"Yes, August. I am." His eyes meet mine. He knows this nightmare has just come true.

August's eyes are drilling me. I want to tell him how stupid I feel for giving up a marriage that meant more to me than my own life. But I keep my truth to myself. Letting him in would do nothing but bring more pain.

Regret finally found its way to me. I should've seen it coming. I should have known this would happen. I would've tried to prepare for the pressure it's putting on me. But I'm rarely prepared for anything this life gives me.

This is by far the worst I've encountered. The *what-ifs* and the *never wills* flood my mind with too many missed opportunities—too many missed memories. I can't change what happened. I try to pull away from the regret, but easier said than done, especially when I'm looking into August's eyes.

Tatum is my husband and always will be. He's my soul mate. *He's my soul mate.* Why does that make me cringe? Why do I want to, so desperately, stay with a man who makes me cringe? *How do I stay with a man who makes me cringe?*

August's stare doesn't waver. His eyes, still glued to me, whisper words that don't need to come from his mouth. I understand what they're saying. But I don't say anything back. The clock for our love ran out a long time ago. We'll never be anything more than expired lovers.

I gulp a big sip of my coffee. He does the same. "I have to get going," he says. *Finally*. "It was nice to see you, Sadie." I wish I could say the same. He flashes me a gentle smile and waves good-bye. *See you around, August.*

My hands wrap themselves around my coffee, absorbing its comfort. And while my mind is off traveling to different time zones, I feel the gentle touch of a finger drag itself from my left shoulder to my right.

"Hey girl," My shoulders collapse when I see Wiley's face. I jump to my feet and wrap myself in her. She's only visiting for a few days, so I want to enjoy her while I can.

Wiley is a light in a room shed with darkness. She's inspired me to try and live my truth throughout the years, but somewhere along the line, I always get lost and end up back where I started.

She knows my feelings for Tatum. She understands them. And even though she lives across the country, she was there the last time Tatum and I's marriage almost ended. She witnessed everything. She knows our marriage is wrong and she has no problem filling me in on what I try so hard to deny.

Today I fill her in on the latest. She bites her lip, sips her coffee, and scrunches her eyebrows as she listens. I can see my words absorbing into her as she cultivates opinions and thoughts that she'll un-regrettably share with me.

Wiley lets out a sigh and takes the final sip of her coffee. "You know what I'm going to say." I roll my eyes at the truth. "I tell my sister the same thing all the time. Happiness trumps your past." She's the only one who knows why I did what I did. The only one who knows my decision to be with Tatum wasn't one I made with a conscious mind. But she doesn't understand my unforgiving need to stay with him. She takes a bite of her buttered croissant. "Tatum isn't a lover. I don't even think he's that great of a person," she says. "I hate to rub it in your face, but you deserve a man like August. Someone who will give back what you put in." My stomach sinks when she says his name.

"I've been through the whole divorce thing before. I can't do it again. What would people think?" I shrug.

"Last time you had someone waiting for you on the other side." She perks her lips. "Admit it. You hate being alone." I shake my head. She's so far off track.

"We were happy in the beginning. We just need to find that again." I take a sip of my coffee. "Our *mojo*."

She tilts her head. "Do you actually believe that or do you feel guilty leaving the man you committed adultery with?" I narrow my eyes. It's guilt, yes, but that's not the core of it. But she doesn't know that and I can't admit that. "Don't settle, Sadie."

Don't settle.

Easier said than done, Wiley.

My driveway's turned into an eerie, dark ally way. The other side is unknown. I'm afraid of my own house. Sin waits for me inside. Issues I've been avoiding sit on the windowsill and wave me in—they don't do a good job. The only thing shoving me out of the car door is my hope.

My hand reaches for the doorknob. It's cold and unwelcoming. I close my eyes and breathe in a breath to help steady my stance. My eyes open and now Tatum's in front of me. His face is long and brimming with disgrace. His arms cradle me before I can even step inside. "I'm so sorry." My arms hang by my side, leaving him to this moment alone. "Babe," he cries. "I'm—I love you." He sputters out nonsense for me to grasp, but it falls to a place I can't reach.

His eyes, puffy and red, search for recognition in mine. "Do you?" I ask. It's the first thing that comes out. The words are so sharp they almost slice my own tongue.

"I was caught up in the moment," he admits. "We haven't said those words...we haven't said those words in who knows how long. I was frozen." He grabs my hand and pulls me inside. He shuts the door behind me. His thumb rubs the rim of mine. I'm not sure if it's my own guilt-ridden mind forcing me to believe his words, or if I actually do.

I stare at him with nothing to give. He's getting closer. And closer. His lips take the final action. Yet still, I stay frozen. "Can you forgive me?" He asks. But what else can I say besides *yes?*

FIVE
Harper

My office desk is a cluttered mess, much like the thoughts combing my mind. People walk back and forth, relaying the same message to too many different people.

I stop and breathe. *I need to breathe.* I never wanted to spend my life working in an office crowded with too many people. But then again, who does?

"Harper?" I don't realize my eyes are closed until I need to open them. They widen—in shock and in fear.

"What the hell are you doing here?" He steps closer to me. His eyes steady on mine. "Tatum." My voice turns to a whisper. "What are you doing?" He shuts the door behind him.

"I couldn't stop thinking about you," he says. "Your lips, the way you taste." His voice is low, sultry. He takes another step closer. My stare is heavy on the way his body moves. It's calling me to come closer, but my feet are rooted in the floor below me.

I bite my bottom lip. He's so close. *So close.* His hands reach out and console my waist, pulling me so there's no space left between us. He dives into my mouth with one thing on his mind. But I don't seem to care.

I want him.

Dear Tatum

I need him.

He lifts me onto my desk and starts to unbutton his pants. Are we really going to do this in my office? *Yes, yes we are.*

"Harper," he whispers. I like the way my name rolls off his tongue. A loud moan escapes my lips when my body takes what he's giving. I forgot how good it feels to be with a man. I grip his shirt and throw my head back. "Harper," he says again.

"Harper," his voice sharpens. "Hey, Harper. Wake up!" *What?* Small specks of light shine in destroying what I thought was real life. *Ugh.*

Lou's staring at me, tapping her wrist. "What?" I ask. It's too bright to want to open my eyes all the way.

"Carson didn't come home from work last night." Her words stab me with no remorse.

"What are you talking about? She's not in her bed?" She shakes her head no. *Damn it.* Panic rides me. My worst nightmare has just come true. My daughter is gone.

I call her phone over and over and over again, getting the same response every time. "This is Carson. Leave a message."

"Carson, answer your phone. Where the hell are you?" My voice, strained and raspy, continues to leave the same message dozens of times.

"Mom?" The moment I hear her voice the panic calms, but rage decides to take over.

"Where the hell are you?"

"Chill. I'm at Noah's. I'm fine." Her voice is stagnant and foul.

"You should've told me."

"Yeah? Well, you've should've noticed long before now that I wasn't home." I roll my eyes at her nasty attempt to make me feel bad.

"Just get the hell home," I say.

I stumble down the stairs and the promise of caffeine dressing my tongue puts me in somewhat of a better mood. I open the lid to the sugar and notice what shouldn't be there. My nose scrunches as I pick her watch out of the sugar bowl. "Why is this in here?" I start to laugh, but when I turn around, watch in hand,

I see shame covering my mom's face. She's cowering, hiding to rid the humiliation. She has no idea how it got there, or why. The words *"I'm so sorry"* repeat over and over again.

A dark message consumes her, pointing at me to come closer. It's a message I should've opened a long time ago. But I've been too selfish. I push it out as far as I can, just so I don't have to deal with the repercussions—the dangers this life can bring. "It's okay, Ma." I try to brush it off as if it's another mistake of old age. But she's pacing back and forth with her walker, fixating on how unsettling this feels. Not even she can understand her mistake.

Her confusion takes my mind off of Tatum for a moment. The thought of kissing him—*a man*—has put question on everything I thought I knew about myself. Everything I thought I knew is...*gone*.

Everything feels chaotic.
Uncontrollable.
Violent.

Admitting a disease has taken control of my mother frightens me. It's something she can't control. It's something *I* can't control. What will it be like if she forgets who I am? Will everything get harder or will our relationship somehow find a way to make amends?

It's selfish to think it may be a second chance to be her daughter, and for her to love me. Maybe she'll see me for who I am and not for being everything she hoped I wouldn't be. *I breathe in*. It'll never be what I've always wished we were.

Her eyes, frail and full of concern, wander the kitchen. They're looking around as if nothing is familiar, as if this isn't the very spot she saw my father choke me, *almost*, to death. I wonder what's being said to her by the voices inside her head. Why do diseases like this surface? Why do they insist on taking away the people we care so much about?

"Are you hungry?" I ask.

"I think so." I don't hesitate to fix her a plate of anything that's easy. Toast is usually her go-to. I press the toaster button down. All that accompanies us is the sizzling of its top layer burning. *Pop.* It's done. Now it's silence that stands between us.

I place a butter knife in front of her with the butter next to it. She usually butters her own toast. She's particular with how much she likes. I sit across from her again and plunge my sight towards her hands. Stiff. Robotic. Harsh. They barely move. She *can't* butter her toast.

She needs me now and I'm here. Right here. I'm right in front of her staring directly into her hollow eyes. And when my father rooted himself in this very spot, I needed her. I stared into her eyes screaming in silence, begging for her help. But she looked away. She blinded herself from what was happening right in front of her. She didn't care enough to help me.

So, why do I run and jump for her?

She never wanted to help.

Ever.

I can't see his face, but I can feel the heat burning off of him. He's ashamed of who his daughter is. I embarrassed him. I embarrassed our entire family.

"Do you understand that being gay is a sin? It should never be a thought that crosses your mind."

"Dad, I—" He steps closer. The sound of his shoes is deafening. My mom's eyes lower to the floor. Her hand creeps away from mine. She knows what's coming next.

His long fingers grip the back of my neck. It's painful, but I can tolerate it. I won't show the hurt—I can't. "It's a yes or no answer, Harper." To promise him I won't be who I am is not an easy task. It doesn't come out naturally. It doesn't want to come out at all. "You laid your lips on her. Her mother is disgusted. I *am disgusted." I gulp. Still, my mom sits and does nothing.*

Silence prevails. His grip has softened. My mom looks up, finally. I wait for her to defend me, but the words that come out are anything but. "It's a phase." That's all she says.

It's. A. Phase. But what if it's not?

The damage still lingers. It teeters back and forth. I try to lean towards the better side of things. And even though we're still so far apart, I'm trying to inch closer. *Trying*. Before it's too late—before the *what-if's* come out to play.

She taps her fingers against the very table we sat at over thirty years ago.

Tap.

Tap.

Tap.

Silence screams our names. But only I can hear the words it's deciding to spiel. *Tap*. She stares at her toast. *Tap*. I stare at her. *Tap*. She has no idea. We've been dancing this dance for too long.

My phone interrupts our merry-go-round. I check to see who's calling, but it's not a number I recognize. I send it to voicemail. I'll listen later.

But it rings again and pushes away my patience. "Hello?" A smile surfaces when I realize who's on the other end of the phone. "Hi, Brandy."

"Have time to meet up?"

I look at my mom. She's still dancing the dance and I'm exhausted from the game. "Yes."

We meet at Local, our favorite high school bar. It's done a terrible job of keeping up with the times, but I enjoy it. It's nostalgic.

I look around and don't see her anywhere. I remember she's never on time. Clearly that trait has followed her into her older years, so I find us a table and wait.

Ten minutes pass and still, she's not here. I call her only to get forwarded to voice mail. I exhale a large breath, hoping she didn't just stand me up. But what would be the purpose?

The door opens and I look up. There she is. She walks over with a lingering smirk. "I am *so* sorry." She drops her bag to the ground and takes a seat. "You'll never guess who I just bumped into." I shrug. "*Wren.*"

Dear Tatum

"No fucking way." What are the odds of that? For thirty years I've been stuck in this town and never, not once, have I ran into someone from high school.

"She's pissed at Tatum." I roll my eyes, un-amused to hear his name. "Supposedly, he ditched her the night of the reunion to come hang with us."

I laugh. "She should have come."

"That's what I told her. She said she didn't feel like entertaining. Whatever that means." Entertain *who*? I wonder what she meant. "Whatever." Brandy brushes it off. "I came here to talk to you about Tatum, missy. How were you not going to tell me?" My heart skips a beat when I piece together the words she's saying.

"I—What? What are you talking about?"

"I know about the kiss. He told me." She reaches her arms out. "Don't worry, I'm not going to say anything. And I haven't told anyone." She zips her lips and throws out the key. I laugh even though deep down I really, really, don't want to. I swallow the humiliation that follows her words. I try to calm the storm that's brewing inside of me. He had no right to tell *anyone*.

Kissing a man isn't something I was ever going to admit out loud. "Well?" She wants the details. "Did you like it?"

"I don't know," I say, knowing that's not true.

"And this is exactly why I'm glad he told me." She shakes her head. "You love to do this to yourself."

"What are you talking about?"

"You suffer in silence, and I won't let that happen again," she says. "Your mind is too loud and your mouth is too quiet."

My lips press together. "I'm happy to have you back." Her eyes sink when she hears the words I needed to say, but her hands squeeze mine, confirming she feels the same way.

"I love you so much, Harper. I would literally do *anything* for you."

My eyes burn from the sting of my tears. They're branding my face as my thoughts stampede through my mind to torture me. I can't stay at home. I won't stay. I can't promise my parents I'll be who they want me to be.

I can't sleep.

My nights are drawn out.

I'm kept up.

I need to leave.

I sneak out the back door before my father makes his way upstairs at his normal time. I have my backpack filled with stuff I'll need to survive. I don't know how long I'll be gone.

I stop by Brandy's bedroom window. I pick up any small pebble I can find to throw, hoping she'll hear me. She pokes her head out. "What the hell are you doing?"

"Leaving," I say in a loud whisper. I don't want her parents to wake up. I don't want them to send me back home. She holds a finger up and vanishes from the window.

Two minutes later she's climbing out with her own backpack. "You're really coming?"

"I'm not letting you go alone," she snaps. "Where are we going anyway?" I shouldn't be surprised. It's not like Brandy has the best life either. Her parents are drunks and if they aren't fighting, they're sleeping on the couch with drool slipping down their chin.

I shrug. "Anywhere, but home."

"Tatum wants your number." My back straightens and I adjust in my seat. *Oh?* Her eyes penetrate me, burning the surface of my skin. She's not patient. "Can I give it to him?"

"Sure."

She tilts her head. "Are you even interested? Because the way he explained it, it—"

"Really?" I sigh. "He went into detail?" She shakes her head. "I just—I don't know. It's weird. This entire thing is weird. I don't know why I enjoyed the kiss as much as I did, but there was a feeling there."

Dear Tatum

"So?" She's trying to coerce me. "If you want to try it out, then go for it. See where it lands you."

I sigh, and then nod. I think I'd like to know more about Tatum. *More about him—and me.*

Together.

I wonder what it would be like to hold someone's hand when walking down the street without any eyes judging us, with no parents hiding their kid's faces. I wonder what it feels like to be *normal*.

She slips me his number too. "Maybe you'll shock yourself." *Maybe.*

It doesn't take long for his number to etch itself into my mind. *What if* I call him? *What if* he answers? *What if* we hit it off? *What if* we don't? So many what-if's—too many. But no matter what my mind is telling me now, the urge to hear his voice continues to grow. But I wait for him.

I walk into the house to one too many voices. I'm not ready to face everyone who's here. And I'm especially not in the mood to deal with Carson's attitude.

A deep breath flows through my nose before opening the door. One foot in front of the other. I focus on that. I don't know why family time has to be so draining sometimes.

"Hey, Harper." Noah smiles as I walk in. Carson's laying on the couch with her legs on his. She says nothing.

"Whatchya watchin'?" I ask.

"A movie." Carson's voice is sharp. I roll my eyes and Noah slightly taps her foot encouraging her to be nicer. I want to tell him my daughter doesn't know how to be nice, but I keep my mouth shut. I don't have the effort to argue right now.

"We don't even know." He throws his hands up and laughs. "We found it on Netflix. It's pretty stupid, but it's giving us a good laugh." I like Noah for Carson. He's lighter than her. She chooses to carry a heavy load on her shoulders. She likes to take it out on me and I've tried to help, but I make it worse.

I always make it worse.

I drag my feet upstairs and am haunted by Carson's laugh. She's happier when I'm not around. It can't be more obvious.

I lie in my bed and can't tell if I'm dreading or anticipating Tatum's call. My heart bangs on the inside of my chest as I wonder what he'll say to me.

I wait. I watch the sun go down from my window. The sky turns black. The stars come out. The Earth continues to move.

Nothing.

My eyes lids sit heavy. They're becoming too heavy to keep open. I give in to their need and close them for the night.

Shit. I forgot to set my alarm last night. My boss is going to kill me.

Sitting at my desk, I prepare for yet another day of my normal, boring routine, reminding myself yet again, I've done nothing eventful with my life. My boss walks past my office, peering in. His glance should've cut me open, but I roll my eyes and pretend I didn't see.

My phone rings. Finally, it rings. This is the first time Tatum's popped up today. But when I look to see who's calling, it's Lou's face that pops up.

"Mom!" Her voice is urgent—scared. "Grammy fell." *Shit.*

Lou's eyes are bloodshot and tears stain her face. She grabs my hand and leads me to the bathroom where I find my mom still on the floor.

"Mom, are you okay?" Her eyes are sad. She's slouched in a position that looks nothing short of uncomfortable. But I'm surprised when she starts to laugh. I look at Lou, eyebrows knitted together. She shrugs.

"I can't believe I fell. I'm so sorry," she says, still laughing. It becomes contagious. I'm just glad she's in good spirits. I'm sure this is painful for her on both the physical and mental aspect. So, I start to laugh too. And soon the three of us are laughing together. "I'm sorry Lou! I didn't mean to scare you."

Dear Tatum

"It's okay, Grammy," she says.

"Does anything hurt? Should I call an ambulance or do you think you'll be okay if Lou and I pick you up?"

"Why would you call an ambulance? Just get me up!" I shake my head. Footsteps fall behind Lou. I throw my head back not in the mood to deal with Adam's shit. I always know when my brother is lingering. His footsteps are heavy from the same boots he's been wearing for the past twenty years.

"What the hell is going on?" He asks when he sees our mom on the bathroom floor.

"She fell, what does it look like?"

"Oh, I'm fine. Just help me up," she banters. So we do.

"Where is her nurse?" His voice goes right through me. It's accusing—always accusing.

"I'd like to know the same thing," I say. "Mom, what happened anyway?"

"With what?" She asks.

"How did you fall?" Adam's voice shortens.

She narrows her eyes and tilts her head. "I didn't fall." Irritation pokes at her voice. I take a deep breath and rub my palm to my forehead.

"Will you stay with her?" I turn to Adam, hating that I have to ask him for help.

"Well, who else is going to do it?" Have I mentioned that I hate him? *Because I do*. So. Much. I roll my eyes and jump in my car and of course, what do I find the moment I sit down? A spaghetti stain on my shirt. Wonderful.

I come out of my room and hear Carson's door open. "Morning." I tilt my head around the corner to find Noah frozen. "You slept here?" He gnaws on his bottom lip and nods.

"I'm sorry, Harper. Carson promised you wouldn't find out and now I'm really regretting my decision and I don't know what to do now and I'm sure you hate—"

"I'm going to work. Don't sleep here ever again. Understood?" He shakes his head yes, very, *very* fast.

I'm almost out of the door when I feel Adam's hand grab me. "Excuse me." I pull away and stare at him.

"Did she *really* fall, Harper?"

"What the fuck are you talking about, Adam?"

"If Ma is unsafe here, then I need to do something."

"I was at work when it happened. See something, say something," I sneer. "I have to go."

SIX
Sadie

Tatum yells my name up the stairs. "Come down here!" I jump out of the shower, soap still in my hair.

"What's wrong?" I'm halfway down the stairs, trying to slow my pace so I don't slip. He looks at the suds on my head and laughs. He hands me a letter. My eyes scan the words scrawled across the paper. *Congratulations*. A smile manages to peak out the sides of my lips, though I should be jumping into his arms, shoving my tongue down his throat. But it doesn't come naturally and I'm not going to force it. I can't fake anymore if I want things to change.

I lean in for a hug and congratulate him. He picks me up and swings me around. My towel nearly falls off as he leans deeper into me. He tugs on it *without* my permission. I step back and fix myself. I haven't been able to go back into that place with him yet. "I'm happy for you, Tatum," I say, hoping it distances his mind from what he's trying to push. "So what's next?" I shrug.

Being invited to the largest medical convention in the country has been a dream of his since before we were married. This can change everything for him. For us. For our family. I want Tatum to be happy. I want to be happy. I want *us* to be happy—

together. So, maybe this can bring us whatever we seem to be missing. Whatever it is. *Whatever has left us.*

If all goes well, his company can grow into something much bigger than what it is. Hopefully leaving him with more money to hire someone to do his job, leaving him with more time for our family.

"I have to go up every month or every other." He knits his eyebrows together trying to remember exactly what he read. "I'll have to look at the email they sent me. But I have to fly up there tomorrow for a formal interview." He scrunches his face again. "Well, it's more of a meet and greet than an interview. They want to meet face to face and take a copy of my license and some of my certificates." *Tomorrow?* My eyes widen. He never listens. Ever.

"You can't possibly be serious," I say. "Charlotte's graduation is tomorrow." He shrugs his shoulders and notes his mistake, though I'm not sure he'll do anything about it.

"She's in fifth grade," he says, trying to take away from her accomplishment. It's hard to believe he doesn't care. "I'm sorry, but I can't risk losing my spot." His words make me shudder. His apology is nothing more than a confirmation of his lack of empathy. It's disgusting.

"There has to be another day you can go. Even if you're a day late," I say. "Tatum. This is a big deal for Charlotte. How are you going to miss this?" It's almost as if I'm begging him to celebrate his own daughter. I'm trying to drill the importance of tomorrow into his head, but steel is too hard to drill.

His priorities are baffling. Anticipation has been chewing at me for the last month. This is a day I'd never miss. Not for work, not for anything. Nothing can stop me from celebrating my daughter. But Tatum? He has his eyes on his own prize. Everything else comes second to him.

"I'm sorry," he says.

"You should be apologizing to her, not me." I bite my bottom lip. "Explain to her why you're already choosing this over her."

"I'm doing this for our family." His voice is low, deeper than normal. But his excuses are nothing more than that.

Dear Tatum

His phone vibrates on the kitchen counter, three times. He rushes over to ensure he gets to it before I do. "Must be the new boss." Sarcasm spills off my tongue. Tatum stays silent. I go back to my shower.

Pregnancy feels like another worldly dimension. Two heartbeats in one body. Some days I feel like I can conquer the world, while other days I feel like the only thing I can do is throw up in the pan next to my bed. Today is one of those days.

I stare at the clock ready for Tatum to come home. One more hour. *The baby has finally started kicking enough to feel it outside of my belly and Tatum's going to flip. At least, I hope he will. I hope feeling her kick will encourage his excitement for our family's newest addition.*

My phone vibrates. I get excited, hoping it's him telling me he's on his way home. But instead of sighing with relief, I find myself rolling my eyes at the words scrawled across the screen.

Staying late tonight. Sorry.

I don't bother responding. I've only been harassing him for the past month to spend more time with me. I need help. And I'm not a clingy person, but it's difficult being on bed rest with no help.

Putting my physical needs aside, I miss him. I really, really miss him. Pregnancy is so hard, yet so incredibly magical. But I need my partner to share this experience with. I crave his promise to help me through this. I crave the warmth of his touch and the feeling of melting into him when his lips meet mine.

And I'm grateful to be able to bare our child, but this is by far the hardest thing I've had to withstand. I need my husband. I want my husband. But even when he's around, his mind is never with us.

Please come home.
Please, Tatum.
Just come home.

SEVEN
Harper

It's been four days and there's still no sign of Tatum. I keep finding myself dialing his number just to erase it. The constant back and forth is becoming exhausting. So, for the last time, I dial his number.

I gulp down the threat inching its way up my throat. The phone starts to ring. Each dial shakes the steady pace of my heart. Pinches of turbulence shake my humanity and what I once saw for myself. I'm not who I thought I was and I don't know how that makes me feel. And...I don't know if the dial tone will ever stop.

Until it does.

He answers. We're connected, *again*. My heart is in my throat—actually, I think it's vomit. "Sorry I told Brandy." It's the first thing he says before saying hi. It brings a smile to my face and settles some of the ache in my stomach.

I wonder if I should call him out on not calling first, but I'm afraid it'll come off more bitchy than funny. "I don't want to lead you on or make you feel like my guinea pig," I say. "But I can't stop thinking about you." The line is quiet. That was my leap of faith. Will life laugh or will it help me up? "Brandy told me you wanted my number," I say, hoping it'll make this a little less awkward. "I thought maybe you wanted to talk."

"I told her we kissed."

"That's it?"

"That's it." His voice trails off as if this isn't something he wanted.

My heart is in my throat and I press my palm to my forehead. I never should've done this. "Well, then I'm sorry I called," I say.

"What? Why? I'm really happy you did," he says. My cheeks bloom into a rosy pink color when he tells me wants to see me again. "I haven't been able to stop the replay of our kiss in my head." There's a smile to his voice now. I bow my head and hide my smile, even though I know he can't see me. "I'm not sure if this is too soon, but I have a work meeting up there in two days if you want to meet up." *Two days?* Is that too soon? My lungs empty the air I need in order to breathe, and catching my breath now seems to be an impossible task. I clench my shirt, close my eyes and inhale through my nose.

Gulping down my anxieties I say, "let's do that."

We don't talk much about the distance lingering between us. And if I'm being honest, I think it's the main reason I'm entertaining this idea. I can experiment without worrying about a trail of gossip to follow.

My thumbs tap the screen of my phone more often now that Tatum's in my life. I immerse myself into the words he shares—the stories he tells. He'll be here tomorrow, but we can't find it in us to end the flow of conversation.

Both of us can vent without the worry of judgment. There's a way about him that makes it easy to talk. All my life I've had to listen to others on what I do and who I sleep with. They've tried to quiet my voice for as long as I could talk. But he makes me feel like the words I share are worthy of someone else's ears.

"Do you want me to pick you up from the airport?"

"I can't ask that of you," he says, politely.

"I can take a half-day at work and pick you up. We can make a day of it." Sweat beads on my hands when I realize how eager I sound.

"I'd love that," he says. "And if you want... you can stay with me at the hotel, too." Part of me hates that just made me smile because I don't know what this feeling is yet. Have I created an illusion? Was it the alcohol that concocted a fantasy for me to live in? Or is this real?

I walk down the stairs unsurprised to see Carson sitting on her phone. "Hey. What's up?" I ask.

"Nothing. What's up?"

"Will you be able to stay with grandma this weekend?" My voice shakes.

She rolls her eyes. "Can't you ask Lou?"

"She's going away."

A harsh breath shoots out of her nose. She wants to say no. I don't blame her. I hate that I have to ask my daughter to take care of her grandmother, but we can't afford nurses on the weekend. We live paycheck to paycheck, and Adam is useless.

She sighs, but agrees. Watching her go on her phone to cancel whatever plans she had makes my skin crawl. "Where are you going anyway?" She probes. I stall. I hadn't thought about this moment. And I don't know what to say. No one, not even my kids know about Tatum.

"Some stupid work conference my boss needs me to go to. It was a last-minute thing."

She doesn't even bat an eye. "Have fun," she says. And just like that, she's back on her phone, avoiding me at all costs.

"Have fun where?" Adam asks. I kick myself for not hearing him come in. These aren't things I tell him, mostly because he loves to give me shit. In his own words, 'the moment you decided to move in, is the moment you decided to live and breathe for her.' *Her as in our mother. Our. Mother.*

"Work conference. Is that allowed?" I narrow my gaze when I look at him. My eyes are my only shield. They can tell him to

Dear Tatum

back off without me having to say the words that'll get me into trouble. His jaw clenches and he narrows his eyes with mine. He draws a fist only I can see. He wants to scream, but our audience won't permit.

"I'll see you guys on Sunday," I say, rushing out the door. I don't know if I'm going to spend the entire weekend with Tatum. I don't even know if I'm going to spend the night, but I rather be prepared.

The airport is insane. Hundreds of people walk out of the same doors and face after face, they all start to look alike. There are so many faces I start to worry I won't notice Tatum's.

Of course I'll notice Tatum, right? Dirty blonde hair. *Perfect lips.* I'm trying to imagine his lips on mine. *He backs away without the urge to pull me back in. Sober. Alone.*

A frustrated moan seeps out. My nerves trickle anxiety through my veins. I look down and hope my outfit is good enough. I even spray an extra pump of perfume. My hands clam up and suddenly I don't know if I can do this.

Breathe in.
Breathe out.
Breathe in.
Breathe out.

I open my eyes and they focus right on the man I'm waiting for. He's smiling, actually smiling. My shoulders begin to relax. I drown in the pleasure he gives off. My anxiety is slipping away, *for now.*

He sees me and runs over. I go to get out, but he jumps in before I can make it. His smile seems permanent. It hasn't wavered once. It's cheesy and big.

Neither one of us can find the right words to say. We're quiet, but it's not awkward. It's almost symphonic. Our eyes are bolted to each other. His are wide and open and the rest of his face is a blur.

His eyes embody a glass wall, showing me what's on the other side. His feelings dance toward me. Elation flows effortlessly. Everything I've worried about is no longer existent in my mind.

He's leaning into me now, lips first. This is the day my heart beats on the outside of my chest, killing me from the blood lost. *It's happening.*

Any moment I'll know if the flare is still lit or if our kiss was just another moment in time. My anxiety whispers in my ear again. *Shit.* He's close and only getting closer. "How was your flight?" I interrupt the moment. We have the entire weekend together. I don't want it to be ruined by a kiss that makes me feel nothing.

He notes what I did. But I'm enjoying what we have now. He falls back into his seat with a rush of air escaping his nostrils. I don't ask what's wrong. I pretend he's tired from the flight.

I hurry to turn the car on. I don't want any empty moments. I don't want either of us to have enough time to second-guess what we're doing. And I don't want to have to turn him down again.

He's ranting about the guy who sat behind him, kicking the back of his seat the entire flight. I give him props for not making a scene. I don't think I'd have enough will power not to.

Standing in front of the hotel desk makes everything feel...*real.* It's a fancy hotel. It's nicer than anything I've ever stayed at. I know I can't afford this place, but I hold my credit card out anyway. My stomach pits when the lady goes to grab it, but Tatum steps in before she reaches it. "I got it," he laughs. I don't know why he laughed, but I'm glad they took his card.

"You sure?" I ask. He nods. I feel a settlement of discomfort crowding my stomach. I already don't feel like I'm enough of a woman to be with him. I don't have money like him. I don't have my own business. I can barely afford my rent now, living with my mother might I add—let alone *two* houses.

I wanted this to be my treat, but he's not used to the things I'm used to. And mediocre hotels are one of them. So yeah, call me selfish. Allow me to wish he'd pay for this instead of me.

Dear Tatum

The door opens to a room I never could've imagined. The walls are glass and mirrored. The skyline line's the room. And it's bigger than my last apartment.

Tatum comes up behind me and cradles me in his arms. His warm breath bounces off the back of my neck. He's comfortable right here, while I'm trying to be calm. It's not his arms hugging me that scare me away. It's the thought of it not scaring me that's terrifying me most.

We stand like this for a couple of moments as I watch the cars and people below us. They're scattering, rummaging, and trying to find the place they need to be. Some are even exploring, while others know exactly where they need to go. I'm reminded of being not so put together. I have so many things left to explore, to find, and to experience.

I turn to face him. His lips, parted and moist, inch towards mine. We're swallowed by silence and our eyes are just as bolted as before. My tongue is tied and my body stiffens.

He's something I need to explore.

The urge to say something, anything, blisters the back of my throat. I don't know what to say, but I need to say something. "Tatum," I whisper. It comes out rough and raspy. I clear my throat.

He runs his thumb along my bottom lip without wavering our stare. "I like you, Harper," he whispers. I rest my arms around his waist and close my eyes.

"I like you." I open my eyes, again. "But I'm—" I stop. He knows who I am. I don't need to say it out loud. "I just don't want to be your fantasy." The words echo inside my head. I've had many men want to turn me straight. It's a painful feeling to navigate.

"You're not a fantasy," he says. My head falls, but he lifts my chin with his finger holding this position. Our lips, only centimeters apart, reach for comfort. His warm breath now hits the skin of my lips, promising more.

His eyes focus on my lips before saying, "I enjoyed your company that night. Kiss or no kiss, I felt like I could be myself." I smile but lean away. He moves in closer without even realizing it. Fear plays against me. Am I wishing for simplicity? Normality? Was it my father who created this mess? Or am I trying to prove to myself that I can be normal? Whatever that means.

My eyelids are heavy. I hate that I won't allow myself to enjoy his company. Tatum brings me in closer. His body warms me. It consumes me completely, collapsing me to dust. I owe it to myself to explore with what time I have left. I owe it to myself to be happy. If Tatum's the one I've been missing, I don't want to let that slip away.

I lean back to look at him. His eyes, deep and dark, penetrate the broken link of my gaze.

I fall for him.
My lips press against his.
His against mine.
Butterflies dance inside my stomach.
It's the feeling I needed to feel.
It confirms everything.
It wasn't the alcohol.

Tatum leans in deeper, pressing his body into mine. His chest moves up and down in a steady, yet exhilarating pace. I grip a fist full of his t-shirt as I push away the urge my body is begging for.

I lean back and my teeth graze my bottom lip, but Tatum doesn't want to stop. His lips travel around my neck leaving a faint trail of saliva along the way. My hands tremble as I work my way around his body. I touch everything except *that*. I learn what his body feels like, where there's muscle, what part craters, even parts that have a little meat to them. It's easy to figure out where he wants this to go. I want it too, but now isn't going to be the time.

Sex is an exceptional part of the relationships I choose to make intimate. But there are parts of my mind that don't allow me to get there easily. There needs to be a comfort blanket for me to feel safe under. I can't expose my entire body for the sake of having some fun. Life has never allowed me to explore sex that

Dear Tatum

way.

My hand gently pushes me away from him. "I'm sorry," I say. I turn around and face the world below us. My eyes swell with tears I won't burden him with.

"I'm not in any rush," he says. "And you shouldn't be either." His hands grip my hips and force me back in his direction. His lips are inches from mine, desperate for another moment to hold them. It's only a thin wall of air that's separating us, yet it feels like a mile of steel. "I want to get to know you." His breath bounces off my lips.

We are so close.

And then we weren't.

"Let's have a drink," he says. I couldn't be more ready to suck something down to help ease this tension.

"I thought you and Wren were married when I ran into you at the reunion," I say as he pours us a drink. He presses his lips together as if it's hard to hold back the laughter building inside of him. He hands me a glass of wine. "Fancy," I laugh.

"Not a wine drinker?"

"I connect more with beer." I shrug. "Or vodka. Definitely vodka."

"I'm surprised you don't know why me and Wren ended." *Surprised?* His eyes find mine, but this time they're murky. They're the same eyes that worried me at the reunion.

"I'm sorry, I—" My stomach knots.

"She kissed someone else," he says. "I was pissed, but in a way it saved me." His eyes go back to normal and the knot in my stomach unties. "She basically blackmailed me into staying with her."

My thoughts stutter and my stomach drops. It's hard to imagine their love wasn't real. It's almost a shame. I was always a little envious of what they had. It's something I've always dreamed of having. "She thought she was superior to everyone else. It was tough having to watch her treat people the way she did," he pauses. "And when I tried to break up with her she threatened to tell everyone my dad had left us." He nods his head in shame. There's hurt in his eyes and it's spilling down his cheeks. "For some reason I was so keen on portraying a perfect life." He stops to catch his breath. "But my family was falling apart and I didn't want to admit it."

Life is filled with cruel games we don't want to play, but need to in order to survive. "Why the change of heart?" I ask. He tilts his head. "I mean at the reunion. Why'd you hang out with her?"

"I was nervous," he says. "Harper, I didn't have a lot of friends in high school, and coming to the reunion was a big deal for me. I wasn't all that comfortable and she was one of the only people I felt comfortable hanging out with." His eyes trail away from mine and reach the city limit. His thoughts scatter his mind.

A soft buzz interrupts his thought. He looks down and holds up a finger as he answers. He steps into the other room, but it's not long before he's back.

"Everything okay?" I ask.

"Yeah. The kids just wanted to say hi." Silence finds us again and I'm okay with it. It's a different kind of silence. It's one I'm not used to. It's one that I feel okay sitting in.

"So," I say. "What happened between you and Sadie? Why didn't you guys work out?" His shoulders deflate as if just thinking about their divorce exhausts him.

"Too many insecurities," he says. "She was always digging to find something I was doing wrong."

"Like what?" I ask.

"Cheating. Sleeping around. Mistress. Thought I was sleeping with my front desk manager, Alisa. Anything and everything you can think of, I was accused of."

"Sounds tiring."

"I would wake up to her face beat red in mine in the middle of the night asking why my laptop was locked up." He shakes his head. "Harper, our house has been robbed before and all of our electronics were stolen. Do the math."

"Are you kidding me? She sounds like a true winner."

"It's too bad. I really loved her, but she let her imagination get the best of her."

"Did you *ever* cheat?"

"No," he says, sticking out his chin. "My dad did it to my mom and that's why our family fell apart."

"I'm sorry that happened." He brings his drink to his lips. He's drinking a mixed drink now. We ordered room service and I finally got my beer.

We fall off the topic of Sadie. I don't want to indulge too much in their past. It is what it is. My past isn't pretty either. I have horror stories that can last for days if I try to tell them.

Tatum is Tatum. I am me. And we're both accepting of these facts. It's what brought us to this space. It's what brought us together.

EIGHT
Sadie

I stand amongst the crowd of parents who seem to be gossiping more than they should be—staring and whispering harsh nothings about other kids outside their *clique*.

It's hard to mingle when people around you are so different than what you stand for. I wish Tatum were here. He'd be someone to talk to. Well, that's if he wasn't sitting on his phone the entire time. I watch Charlotte run with her friends. It's their last hurrah before venturing into middle school. I think Tatum's going to regret not coming.

I hope he regrets not coming.

"Sadie!" A voice from behind me screams my name. I almost don't want to look back. I'm far from the mood of bearing the art of chitchat. "Sadie." The voice gets closer, too close for me to ignore.

"Wiley?" Why didn't I think she'd be here? Wiley's always coming through for the people she loves most. Her late husband Alex has a niece that goes to school with Charlotte. Wiley's always been close with his family, so I shouldn't be surprised she's here. "I've been calling you to tell you I was coming."

"I'm so sorry," I say. "Tatum left and I've been dealing with the kids on my own and—"

"He left? To go where?"

"Leavenworth," I shrug.

She rolls her eyes. "I hope for good reason."

"Medical convention."

She ignores my response. She hates his excuses almost as much as I do. "Why don't you come over Alex's sister's house?" Her eyes aren't begging, but they're telling me to say yes.

I decline anyway. The energy living in my body isn't enough to sustain a fifth-grade graduation party. "Sadie, come on. Tatum's gone, live for a moment. Even if it's just for tonight." Maybe she's right. Maybe it'll be better than going home to an empty house to sit alone in a puddle of disturbing thoughts.

My head falls back and I let out a sigh, and then yell for Charlotte. We're going. We need to go, even if it's only for my mental well-being.

The vicious guard dog that lies at the end of the driveway jumps up ready to attack our car. His tail wags faster than our eyes can catch. He waits to attack us with his slobbery tongue, and Charlotte doesn't hesitate to jump out and embrace the licks of this forty-pound fur ball.

Wiley meets us at the door, greeting me with a much-needed glass of wine. "I thought you'd need this." She smirks and purses her lips.

"Just when I thought you couldn't get any better." I raise the glass right before taking a generous sip. But it's going to take more than one to release the tension building in my spine. Another gulp eases its way down my throat, emptying my glass before I even make it inside.

I turn the corner, heading straight for the kitchen. A pair of eyes narrow in on me and begin to scratch the surface of my skin. Two weights rest on my shoulders and suddenly I fall weak. My wine glass shatters all over the floor and my face flushes with lingering embarrassment.

I gasp, quietly. My heart drills a hole from the inside out as he continues to stare. "Hi," I finally say. My voice is soft, but I'm sure he heard me. My feet root themselves into the floor below me. August brings himself to his feet. We're not face-to-face or nose-to-nose.

We're six feet apart.

Six feet.

No one notices the line between us. *Thank God.*

He moves a step closer and I break the awkward silence growing between us. "I can't believe I just broke this glass." I laugh, awkwardly.

"Yeah," he says, biting his bottom lip. "There's a sign on the door that says they charge for broken wine glasses." His smirk makes me blush.

I can't say anything before Wiley's next to me with a dustpan. His hand reaches towards me. I'm scared to touch it. I'm scared for our skin to touch—for our skin to remember what we taste like. So instead, I brush off my pants and stand up on my own.

The cages in the back of our minds keep the words we both want to say locked away. His lips maneuver, he's trying to get something out. Something that's hard to say. But his attention is drawn away when one of his friends pulls on his arm. "It's nice to see you here, Sadie," he says.

"Thanks." I turn my back first.

I always turn my back first.

"I am so sorry." Wiley throws her hand down on the counter next to me and sighs. Her jaw clenches together as if she's preparing for me to fight back. "I didn't even realize he was here until I saw the two of you facing each other like awkward long time lovers." I laugh and assure her both August and I are completely at ease with our current situation.

I haven't told her about us bumping into each other at The Coffee Bean the other day. I'm not sure why because Wiley's my person. You know? Like everyone always has a person they tell *everything* too. Even with her living across the country, she knows more about who I am than Tatum.

But every time our encounter replays in my head, I get

Dear Tatum

antsy. I hate thinking about it. I hate thinking about the feeling I got when I saw him. I hate that I got happy to see him. I hate that he was happy to see me.

But what I hate even more than all of that is the spark in Wiley's eyes. I know how she feels about August. And I don't mean her feelings towards him. I mean her feelings towards him and I, *together*.

August is a friend of Alex, Wiley's late husband. We met years ago at a club I shouldn't have been at. I didn't realize August stayed in touch with his family so well. Honestly, if I had known, I never would have showed.

The flashing lights and loud music encourage me to dance. I came alone, so I dance with myself. I'm lost in the movement of my own body and the feeling this drink is giving me. Closing my eyes, I watch the light show my eyelids show off. It hands me a new sense of fairytale. I chug the rest of my drink and allow myself to become a long flow of effortless movement.

I should be focusing on school and work. But this... this takes my mind out of the dark places I choose to hide, the horrors my body puts me through, and the endless ache my body feels. This is where I feel the most normal. I feel like I'm just another twenty something year old with little to no worry.

Coming here often helps ease my mind. The lights flash different narratives through the crowd. Looking around, I catch small glimpses of other people's night and try to imagine being one of them.

I take another careless sip of my drink and bounce off the body of someone else. It's harsh, but an accident. His drink spills all over me, along with my own. "Oh my God," he says. "I'm so sorry." He tries to yell over the music. We both look down at my shirt, my white shirt. I don't know if he's still looking at the disaster we caused or if my low cut top has attracted his attention. "What were you drinking? I'll grab you another one."

I walk with him, not to get to know him, but because it'll be hard to find me again in the sea of people floating around the room. His friends are here waiting for him. They laugh when they find out what happened. I guess he's the clumsy one of the group. "This is Wiley and her boyfriend Alex." I wave.

"Sadie," I say.

"I'm August by the way." I bite my lip. His voice is faint over the music, but I like the way it sounds. Now that I can see him a little bit better, I like how he looks. Charming, but not a playboy. Hot, but not full of himself.

I scan the room to people-watch as I wait for my drink to come. The side door opens and strangely, I make eye contact with the leader of the pack. "Shit." It's Ember, my best friend. She sees me and rage takes over. She shakes her head and walks out of the door she just came in. "I'll be right back."

I run after her and I'm lucky enough to spot her through the crowd of people on the sidewalk. Catching up to her, I grab her arm. "Hey!" She turns around and pulls away from me. "I thought you said you were going to Pablanos tonight."

"And I thought you said you were staying in." Her eyes narrow into small slits.

"It's not what you think," I say, but she doesn't believe me.

"You should start caring more about your health. Drinking every day isn't going to help you and sleeping with that guy isn't going to make him want you."

I laugh before responding. She's scolding me for being at a club she was at. "Ember," I say. "Are you kidding me?" The alcohol serves me no strength to hold back this throbbing laugh sitting in my throat.

"We're here for two different reasons, Sadie." Her eyes dig deeper. "But I don't need to tell you that, do I?" Despite laughing in her face and quite possibly pushing away one of my best friends, she's right. I care way too little about my health. Doing this night after night won't promise me strength. But purposely destroying it will give me a reason if it decides to fail me again.

I stop laughing and listen to what her body is telling me. Her eyes hold onto a pain she doesn't want to unleash. Steam pours out *of her. I can see the words she wants to say etched onto her face. But I have nothing else to say and neither does she. She walks away, again, for the last time. I choose not to follow.*

I always choose not to follow.

"Do you still fantasize about him?" My head snaps to face Wiley. My cheeks blush when I see her staring at him from across the room. "Oh, I forgot," she says. "Tatum is your one and only." She sticks her tongue out and I laugh at her.

"Tatum's my husband. August is my ex-husband and we're going to keep it that way." Wiley peers through my outer shell. She knows my truth even without me having to say a single word.

"I still don't understand what went wrong." She's talking about August and I. It's hard for her to understand why I slept with Tatum when August and I were almost near perfect together. But she doesn't know the truth and she wouldn't understand the truth.

No one does.

Not even Tatum.

Sometimes life is just too hard for people to understand. And having to make certain decisions will hurt. It'll hurt like hell. It'll burn and the devil will laugh, but it needs to be done.

August creeps next to me to pour himself a glass of wine. "Refill?" He asks. I push my glass towards him and he fills it until it's about to overflow. "I still remember how full you like your glass." We both laugh, but we look away from each other. It's like we're scared to connect. To touch. To breathe each other's air.

My eyes meet Wiley's, begging for an out. She starts to cheese and I roll my eyes. I lift my glass and allow my taste buds to be spoiled. "I'll leave the two of you alone," she mouths. I cringe as she walks away, leaving me to suffer the presence of August alone.

"So weird that we've run into each other twice this week." He inches towards me.

"Very," I take another sip of my wine, but it needs to be swallowed in two gulps. Sweat starts to swim down the center of my back and suddenly I'm hit with a hot flash. I look around, desperate, to find a corner to hide in.

But August starts to talk again. "You know, Sadie," he says, then takes a sip of his wine. "I often think about our—" *Shit*. This is exactly why I didn't want to be around him. Memories. Reminders. Things to engulf us in our past. I don't want to feel it. I don't want to remember it. And I don't want August to think he has a shot.

We're expired lovers.

I sigh, nervous to let the words flooding my mind out into the open, but I have to. I can't lead him on or even listen to what he's been fantasizing about. "I'm still married to Tatum." The words burn the back of my throat almost as much as they did when I admitted my affair.

His crow's feet start to show. I don't want to know why he's smirking at me like he's going to ramble on despite my push back. But our eyes are finally connected. They're brimming with thought. It's difficult to look away from anything that is as riveting as this. "Why are you smiling?"

"Because the last thing I'd ever do is try to take away what you love," he says. "I care about your happiness." His pinky brushes the side of my hand and my stomach falls.

I don't want to remember what he feels like.

I can't.

"I know you love Tatum and I won't try to ruin that."

I know you love Tatum.

August, if you only knew.

I'm embarrassed for assuming what words were going to spill off his tongue. "I'm sorry," I say. I wish I could tell him the truth. I wish I could tell him that karma has finally found its way to me. That being with Tatum was not what I imagined. And that maybe, *just maybe*, I'll never be happy with him. So instead, I just smile and take another sip of my wine.

A faint laugh escapes his lips. "I was going to say how I often think about how much of an amazing business woman you were in our office." *Often? Our?* "I guess I just need to know if you ever started that business of yours?" I haven't thought about opening my own design company in years. Honestly, I haven't thought about it since we were together. It's not something Tatum values. He needed his business to grow and I needed to be there to support him.

I nod before I open my mouth to tell him no, I never started it. "Thanks," is what comes out. I cower, ashamed I never even tried to follow through with my desired plans. "But I never did." He crinkles his nose and I can see his thoughts scatter. "Well, Tatum ended up starting his own business not too long after we got married. So, I help him with whatever is needed."

"I'd assume that's basically everything." I'm not sure if that's a dig at Tatum or a compliment for me, either way, I don't bother feeding into it.

"Unfortunately, no," I say. "Especially now with my dad's passing. He's given me a lot of time off. And not only that, but he loves to be in control." I shrug.

"I'm so sorry to hear about your dad," he says, ignoring everything else. "That's awful. I'm so sorry," he says again. I hand him a softer smile than I'm used to. "I know it's not my place, but if you need anything, I'm here for you." August saw first hand how I was with my dad. He understood that my mother wasn't always a mother and that my dad was both parents most of the time. "I can't imagine it's been easy on you."

I shrug. "He was old. We had our time together. I have memories. I'll be okay." My words feel honest. For the first time, I don't feel suffocated with guilt for saying just that.

Not having Tatum jumping down my throat telling me how sad I am and how I need mandatory time off, makes me realize how sad I'm actually not. I've given a moment to think without a second voice.

I bite my lip and stare at August from afar. He's turned away talking to another guest. I move closer without notice, grabbing the bottle of wine sitting next to him, and hope he doesn't waver his attention. "Another glass already?" He teases. I gasp a sharp breath in. I wasn't ready to hear his voice.

"Last one of the night." I raise my glass and walk away.

NINE
Sadie

My mind is fuzzy from last night. I had one too many glasses of wine. Forcing myself out of bed, I swing one leg out at a time and shuffle my way to the bathroom.

There are two things I need off my mind, this headache and August. I pop two Advil hoping it'll help—*both*.

I can hear the voices of my children downstairs. "Good morning," I say. The house is brimming with chaos. The T.V. is on, the kids are playing, and the laundry is going. A lot goes on in our house on Saturday mornings, yet strangely, it's easy for me to find comfort in these types of moments.

Soon my Saturday mornings will be quiet. The kids will sleep in or be at a friend's house. I wish Tatum would take more advantage of these times. Even though, deep down, I know the distance between them is my fault.

"Mom," Charlotte yells. "Your phone!"

I have pancake mix dripping from the tips of my fingers, and as much as I hate the taste of the raw mixture, I lick it anyway.

The number across the screen isn't one I recognize, but I decide to answer anyway.

"Hello?"

"Sadie?" The voice on the other end of the phone shakes as their lips form my name. It's not familiar, but then again voices over the phone always sound a bit different. "It's August." My mouth falls open and hangs without movement. *August?* My voice is paralyzed.

"Hi." My voice cracks. Time stops. Sweat drips. All sound is hushed. Anxiety cripples me and strikes me hard in the back of my head.

"I'm crossing a line right now. I know. But I have to ask." *Shit.* I rummage through last night's affairs. Did I lead him on? Did I give mixed signals? I shame myself as a married woman. How could I let this happen again? I've made this mistake before. I can't believe I've done it, again. "Would you be able to meet up at The Coffee Bean later for a cup of our favorite?" A soft laugh echoes his question. But it's hard for me to find the humor in this.

It doesn't matter how badly I want to say yes. *I can't.* I won't. My mind broods thoughts of the past and the future. I fell for this before and I have to live with the consequences every day.

"Um," I hesitate to answer. "I don't think today would work." He hears the doubt in my voice. It's loud and obvious.

"I'm sorry I called." He sounds more upset with himself than with me. He's an honest person, always doing what's morally correct—*most of the time.*

He apologizes again, but the words blur my mind. Flashbacks flood my head. My cheeks burn with past memories. Guilt *always* finds its way back to me.

August is sitting in front of me, his eyes smiling. It's been two days since I met him at the club. He seems happier being here in this restaurant that's filled with lots of different types of people. Families, couples, newlyweds, and two strangers sitting face to face.

"Tell me about yourself," he says. I tilt my head wondering if that's a good thing to do right now. My past is an easy way to scare people—at least that's what I like to think. It's easier than admit-

Dear Tatum

ting I'm the one pushing everyone away.

"My favorite color is blue," I say. He presses his lips together as if he's going to laugh, but doesn't want to show it.

"Anything else?"

"Honestly," I say. "There's a lot I can say, but it's dark." I shrug and take a bite of my salad. "I'd hate to dim our time with my horror stories."

He falls back in his seat and crosses his arms. "I'm all ears." Now I'm the one pressing my lips together.

"Maybe we should save my dark history for another time," I say.

"I'm glad I'm getting another date." He winks and starts talking about all the things we can do. I smile. He's not like the guys I've been with before. He's full of life, something I've been missing.

"Hello?" Tatum's breath is short and hoarse.

"Is everything okay?" I ask.

He assures me it's nothing more than him being almost late for the train. I listen to the sound of his voice. I absorb every word. Every sound his voice makes. It's hard to recognize over the phone. It moves slow but steady.

His sentences lack any comfort for me to lie in. They're short—rushed. I want to miss him. I want him to miss me. But I don't think that's a place we're at. Or maybe I'm just too caught up in my past with August. Since he's been floating around, my mind is colored in a different pattern. Maybe I'm just caught up in the difference of attention.

"I have to go," he says. "I'll try to call later."

Try.

The line goes dead before I can say good-bye. I'm stuffed with empty voids his words have burned me with. The word *try* lingers. He never asked about our family, *his family*.

My eyes burn from staring at August's phone number. Maybe we should meet. My finger floats above the call button. But just as I'm about to call, Tatum's name pops up on the top of my screen. Love you. He writes, forcing me out of my head. I exit out of August's number. I can never, *ever*, call his phone.

TEN
Sadie

I'm back at the airport staring at the same two doors Tatum exited weeks ago. Except for this time, it's pain pinching my heart instead of thrill. It's disappointing that we're here in our marriage. A point where missing him isn't a feeling I'm sure about. I wanted him home, but as I watch him make his way to the car, I'm not sure if here is where I want to be.

He leans over the armrest to hug me. One arm wraps around me while the other lies limp, gripping his phone. *His phone.* I pull back in my seat and start the car.

This dull feeling hurts for more than one reason. Shouldn't excitement be hitting me? Shouldn't a wife miss her husband, no matter how long or short the time spent apart was? *What am I missing?*

He lifts my chin with his index finger. "What's wrong?" He asks, but I don't know the answer.

"We missed you, that's all." I'm not sure if that's the truth or a lie. We did miss him. I just don't miss him now.

"I missed you guys, too," he says. His stare doesn't waver from his phone. "Let's go." He waves his hand. "I have a lot of work to catch up on." I roll my eyes—nothing like catching up on family time. We've missed a shit ton of that lately. But who cares, right?

I face the kitchen window with a hot cup of coffee. Tatum's gone for who knows how long, the kids are at his mom's and I'm left all by myself. *Again.*

All the things I want for our marriage perch onto my shoulders and look up at me. I have a lot of faults. Tons. But the thought of being unhappy for fifteen more years just doesn't sit right. We can't dance like this forever.

I walk into Tatum's office not fully understanding what this will bring us—what it'll bring me. Maybe a lot or maybe nothing at all. But something's calling me to follow, so I have to at least try to give it something.

I walk into silence. The waiting room is vacant. An empty chair fills the front desk. No one's around.

Alisa pops her head out from the back room. "Mrs. Barnes," she says, eyes wide. "What are you doing here?" She fixes her hair and straightens out her pants.

Was she just...?

I don't finish the thought. I like Alisa and the last thing I want is to find out she's banging her boyfriend in the office.

"Just here to see Tatum," I say.

"Not here." She clears her throat. "He's not here today. He doesn't come back until tomorrow." She's acting weird, too weird for me to want to stick around any longer. I can't imagine the feeling of getting caught by the owner's wife. Talk about a tough thing to swallow. Especially when I'm the supposed *office manager.*

But now the question sits, where the hell is he? And why did he lie? Is it me? Am I pushing him away? Is it the stretch marks that stain my body? Have the lines on my face blurred the beauty he once saw? *Does he know the truth?*

I hold out faith that one day the games will end. One day I won't have a constant weight of disappointment filling me. One day I won't have to chase his love.

We need change.

We need effort.

We need to find each other again.

I search on foot, tearing our town apart in hopes to find my marriage again. Place after place. Not leaving a rock unturned. I try not to let the anger control me, but it's hard when that's all I can feel. It devours me without putting in any effort.

I don't know who I should be mad at. Him? Me? Maybe both of us. I'm embarrassed I let this go as far as I have. Am I trying too hard? Am I holding on too tight? I shake the thought.

Think positive.

Think positive.

THINK POSITIVE!

There must be a logical reason for this mess.

I creep up my front steps, exhausted from the day. I don't know if I should expect to see Tatum or if he'll show up at midnight.

But there, right when I walk in is a large bouquet of pink roses sitting on the counter. A note sits ontop and Tatum is still nowhere to be found. They don't make me happy. They don't do what they were supposed to do. My hand tenses around a rose. My grip grows tighter. And tighter. And tighter. *Let it go, Sadie.*

Was this a guilt gift? Fury sparks. I close my eyes and inhale a deep breath to calm my raging thoughts. I holler up the stairs and the sound of footsteps scatter. He has a towel wrapped around his waist and a smile plastered across his face.

"Are you smiling because you washed away the evidence of the woman you just tongued?" I didn't say that, but I wanted too.

"Hey babe," he says.

"Where were you today?" My jaw clenches with my fist. His fingertips find his bottom lip. "Quit the bullshit, Tatum. I know you weren't at work." His shoulders slouch forward and his face relaxes. His lips pout. One stair at a time, he comes down, meeting me in the hallway. He places the blame on me without even talking.

He bows his head then looks up at me. "I didn't want you to find out." My heart sinks. I close my eyes ready to hear the words that will destroy me. "I was looking at venues." *What?* "Our fifteenth wedding anniversary is coming up and I wanted to surprise you with a ceremony to renew our vows." His voice hampers as he presses his lips into a line. "Why do you always want to catch me in a lie?" He swallows hard and his words get tight. "How are you going to catch me now?" He mocks me with pleasure. "You're so swallowed up in the past you won't allow yourself to have a future. Every day you're reminded I can be up to no good." His eyes sink, deepening the circles around his eyes.

This is angry Tatum. This is someone else. He's darker. Quicker. Harsher. He moves to the beat of the devil. His eyes penetrate me. His fists are curled. He's ready to hurt me.

"Calm down," I say in a mulled tone.

His hands finally relax. His eyes are next. I ruined a great surprise. Of course, he's going to be mad. He doesn't say anything more. He storms up the stairs and slams the door.

My body collapses within itself and I feel horrible for digging too deep this time. I pour myself a cup of coffee and watch the steam release itself. I wish my own self-destructive qualities could disappear that easily.

Too many thoughts cloud my judgment. But one thing I know for sure is Tatum's right. I live in the past. The more I think about it, the more I realize I may be the one kicking my marriage into this dark hole. *It's my fault.* The future can't swim in when the dam is closed. It can't help us. It can't heal us. I've been looking in the wrong direction all this time.

It's on me to fix this marriage. And it's on me to make the next move. I open the bedroom door and Tatum looks up at me. Silence swims between us. His grip loosens from the book he's reading when he sees me unbutton my shirt.

I strut towards him slowly, peeling off each layer covering my body. My hips sway side to side. My bra is now being flung to the side of the room. Tatum bites his lip, anticipating what's to come. I don't think he's mad anymore.

Dear Tatum

    He's impatient, always has been. He stands up. I push him back onto the bed, ready to make my next move. He wants this. I want this.

    Maybe this will fix this.

    Maybe this will fix *us*.

ELEVEN
Sadie

Sex isn't a magical tool to fix the needy. It doesn't fulfill your needs and desires if you're empty inside. I learned this the hard way. My veins aren't raging with the stimulation I thought would be here when Tatum inserted himself inside of me. Instead, it's pain tearing through me. Every stroke I thought would heal me, tore me up instead. Every kiss given was only a reminder of what our marriage will never be.

I was wrong, so wrong. Sex will never fix Tatum and I.

He hasn't kissed me since we stopped fucking each other. And I'll stop calling our sex making love because it seems it's stuffed with more savagery than passion. His back is towards me now and I'm left to stare at the hairs that fill the back of his head. It's a view I see far too often.

Distance is hard, especially when you're lying in the same bed. Tatum's two inches from me, but he feels so out of reach. My arms stretch out to touch him, but he moves just in time. I sigh. He got away, again.

I make a point to move closer. I wrap my arm around him and pull myself in to be the big spoon. I fall into the warmth his body gives, but he nudges me away.

Dear Tatum

I bite my bottom lip, somehow hoping that'll stop the tears from falling. But I take the hint and lean back into my crevice.

I can see the light from his phone shining on the ceiling. He's awake. *Thumbs dancing.* I guess now would be a good time to talk about Alisa. Maybe it'll give him something else to think about—something other than whoever is on the other end of that phone.

"I saw Alisa yesterday," I say.

Silence.

"She was having sex."

Still nothing.

"Tatum?"

"What?" He asks.

"Alisa was having sex in the office yesterday."

"Oh," he says. "I'll talk to her about it."

"You'll talk to her about it?"

His voice tightens. "I'll talk to her about it." He doesn't move from the position he's in and doesn't say anything more. *He'll talk to her.* Whatever that means.

I fall into my pillow and stare at the ceiling.

His phone lights up.

He grabs his phone.

His thumbs dance.

He puts down his phone.

The cycle continues. I try not to think about it. I try not to allow my mind to spin in vicious cycles. Focusing on my breathing helps ease the pain.

Tatum's sleeping now. I can hear the soft snores getting louder. It must be nice to disconnect from reality so easily. My eyes refuse to close and like many things, I give up trying.

I scurry down the stairs and satisfy my growing sweet tooth with a bowl of fresh-cut strawberries. I remember when Tatum used to taste like this. During the times we had to sneak around, I'd let the taste of his body linger on my tongue for as long as possible. He used to drive me crazy, in a good way, of course. I miss the giddy feeling he used to give me. But that feeling wasn't made for us. It was never meant to last. At least, that's what it feels like.

I'm drowning in the past again. *Let it go.* This is going to be a hard habit to bite, but in the end, it will have been a habit worth biting for. So, I force myself into something else.

I find myself scrolling aimlessly on my phone. Photos. Messages. Recent calls. *August's recent call.* My eyes are fixated on the same ten numbers that called me a few days ago. I'm scared. I'm scared because I'm having a hard time finding the guilt that should come along with them.

Just meet him for coffee. It's harmless.
Harmless.

I said the same thing ten years ago, which turned out to be nothing short of tragic. But I convince myself that my unruly mistakes were based on my age and my own stupidity.

August can be a friend.
We should be friends.

My eyes shoot to the stairs, which leads to Tatum, which leads to questions, which leads to memories, which leads to pain. A lot of pain. Pain I willingly put myself through every day. I circle it every waking moment we're around each other.

No matter how hard I try not to circle the past, it always shows up. It taunts me. And I'm not sure our marital issues are within our control anymore—*my control*. No matter how hard I try, I might always see the dark instead of what's light. Maybe we're too damaged.

I want to fight for our marriage, but every time I turn around I find myself fighting for a way out. We both have secrets—dark secrets. I'm not perfect, far from it, which is why I stay.

But through my own wrongdoings, I feel it's my responsibility to forgive him for whatever he does behind my back. Because nothing he does can ever amount to what I have done.

All the wrong things trace my mind when I stare at August's phone number. It's easy to think about all that's wrong with Tatum when the thought of August is circling. I tap the number without thinking. *Shit.* I panic for a minute, but let it ring.

Seconds feel like minutes. My eyes are squeezed shut just waiting to hear his voice. Part of me wants his answering machine to pick up, so I can text to apologize for *"accidentally"* calling. Then again, you could consider this an accident. It was my subconscious mind that pressed the button after all.

"Sadie?"

"Hi August," I say. "Sorry for calling so late."

"Not a problem." A laugh echoes his words and without doubt, he jumps into a conversation that I find myself tangled in.

There isn't a rush of excitement when talking to him. I don't feel my emotions running wild or out of control. I'm brought with contentment. My words flow naturally, almost like I don't have to think.

For the first time in a long time, I feel okay. My passion for life comes alive in our conversation. He reminds me of all the promises I made myself. Promises I deprived myself of. *Where did I go wrong?* I know the answer to that question. I can pin the exact moment everything changed.

I close my eyes and watch it play out in front of me. It stings every part of my body. Watching it replay in my head is even worse than when it happened. I hate that I've made so many wrong decisions.

"If you're still up for that coffee, I'd love to meet up," I finally say. He agrees, of course. And when our call ends, my giddy teenager feeling chimes in, but I shove it to the side and go back to bed.

This is harmless.

Without thought, my blouse is torn open. August's lips are stuck to my neck as I try to catch my breath. My hands search the wall in hopes for a steadier grip, but August's hands tie around my waist and lift me onto the bed.

Open and exposed, without a second thought. His pants are ripped off and I see everything—everything I wanted to see, every-

thing I've missed. His finger traces the outline of my body and I'm reminded of his touch, how gentle yet rough it feels. Chills layer my body, sending me into the world I almost forgot existed.

Here lies years of fantasy—years of missing.

His hand lining my body reminds me of what it feels like to be alive again. My body thrives off his touch.

This is what love is.

My back arches as he continues to explore the body of what was once his. He moans when he finds a spot he loves. I moan every time he finds it.

I move naturally to the way his body dances on mine. I follow the river my veins pump and finish in his mouth.

He finishes with me.

In sync.

In tune.

Like we were never apart.

TWELVE
Sadie

Fear kicks us offbeat. It's the unknown that hurts you. It's being convinced of what darkness has in store, promising the worst possible outcome. The what-ifs deluge our thoughts and suffocate us with an answer we don't want to feel.

Fear is sneaky. Its claws emerge from its bony fingers and creep up our back in a silent attack. Holding onto our mouths and controlling our breath brings it to life. *It's taking control.* Yet somehow, we always manage to make it out alive.

I've had the unfortunate pleasure of learning the ins and outs of fear. There are many types of fear out there waiting to devour us during our weakest moments. There's the kind that leaves you in your bed at night wondering what's crawling beneath you, the fear of getting hurt, or making the wrong decision. There's even the fear of making the right decision. What if this makes me happy? *Then what?*

Seeing August scares me. I feel the prick of fear crawling up my back. Too many questions pick at my mind, leaning me towards the wrong side of things.

I shouldn't be here. But I can't leave, especially now that he's seen me.

My hand waves a shaky hello as I tuck my chin into my chest. My past mistakes circle to the point of exhaustion. They're loud and current, screaming sweet nothings into my ear.

August waves with a faint, yet goofy smile, encouraging me to come sit. And I do. His smile comes without shame. He isn't allowing the past to get in the way.

"I got this for you." He nudges a full cup of coffee towards me. I celebrate with a sip and I'm surprised it's exactly how I order it. "I remembered," he says, subtly trying to brag. *Tatum would never.* And I think he knows that.

August starts digging in his pocket. His brows knit as he struggles to pull out a white envelope. "I wanted to give this to you."

"What's this?" I ask. He nudges it closer. "No," I say turning down the stack of blue bills. "Absolutely not."

"For everything I've missed." What kind of person would I be accepting money for something he never had the privilege to experience?

I push it away. Far, far away. It's a disgusting reminder of the sin I promised not to commit. "I can't, August." My throat tightens. "I could never accept this."

Tragedy lingers between us. "Please, Sadie." His hand covers mine, not to feel my skin, but to ease my mind—to tell me it's okay, take the money.

I'd hate to see the look on my face right now. But August doesn't mind it. His eyes drill me. They pull and yank, but his intention isn't to hurt me. It's shame wearing me down into a tiny nub of nothing. My own anger clots in my throat, forcing down the words I need to speak. "I'm sorry," I finally say.

"You did what you had to do to survive, Sadie. I can't knock you for that." And he's right. I did what I needed to keep my family together and for some reason, he's okay with that. At least that's what he says. I can't seem to be convinced.

A part of him must be empty, missing even. It's a piece of him that's lost—a part of him he can't reach. A fraction of discomfort sits quietly in his eyes, yet buried inside of him is the will to forgive.

"You don't get it," I say. "I made the wrong choice." My words spill out like an open dam and I'm unable to stop the flow.

I bow my head and tap my fingers on my forehead. From the corner of my eye, I see August lift his hand to comfort me, but our skin never touches. Instead, he puts his hand back on his lap where it belongs. We both know how wrong this is.

I came here seeking comfort in August, knowing it was wrong. But it wasn't physical comfort I was after. I needed something, *anything*, to convince me my marriage is the right path—something to promise me I've made the right choice.

But yet again, I was wrong.

So, so wrong.

The thought of August gnaws on me. He broadcasts his affection in a way that can't be replicated. It's hard not to wish Tatum were a little bit more like him.

Pure.

    Radiant.

        Durable.

That's the kind of love I need from Tatum—the kind of love I crave. One that's obvious from the outside. I'm holding out hope that he'll come around. It's the only thing I can do.

The room is dark. I'm not sure where he lies on the bed, but I'm okay with it. Just knowing he's near is enough for comfort. He tosses himself over, but our bodies have yet to touch. I want him closer, but I'm nervous. We've yet to tangle ourselves in each other to love the way two lovers do. But tonight may be the night that all changes.

I'm shaken with the thought this might change what we are. But then again, I'm not sure what we are, if anything at all. But I'm sure that August is meant to be someone to me. Why else would he keep popping up?

He moves closer. I can feel his body lining mine. His breath is faint but strong enough to feel. His lips graze the skin of my neck. I gasp and clench the sheets. I want to taste him. I want him to taste me.

Alcohol protrudes off both of us, but it's not intolerable. In fact, it's making the frivolous feeling in the pit of my stomach heat up. I don't want to wait anymore.

This isn't like any other hook up I've battered. We've been on dates. We've bumped into each other at random times. Life keeps bringing him to me, even when I'm trying to pull away.

Shadows cover parts of his face as we roll around the bed. Bits of light shine in at just the right moments. Our eyes will catch a glimpse of the other person. We connect better this way.

My body throbs with the promise of tonight. His hands explore parts of my body that have never been touched. His breath is warm on my skin as we continue to shed our layers.

His mouth is traveling in the opposite direction now. His lips stop every couple inches to savor the moment we're in. He's getting closer. Closer. His lips drive me mad.

I pull him up and he takes notice of what I want and gives it devotedly. He thrusts me, not with lust, but passion. He bows his head and takes control of my lips. His tongue swims in my mouth. His breath is bitter, yet sweet. I like it. Our saliva swaps, but it's not as gross as it sounds.

Gentle is the word that comes to mind—the only word that feels right. There's a desire and need for my body to be cherished. It's the first time someone appreciates what my body has to offer.

August is different.

So, so different.

I pinch my eyes close when I see Tatum sitting on the couch. I take a deep breath. "Hey."

His eyes barely look over at me. "Hi," he says back. I wonder what he's thinking. I wonder if he plans on doing the same dirty deed I've just committed. His fingers take hold of his phone, tight. His thumbs dance. I wonder if it's always the same person on the other end of his phone.

Dear Tatum

"How's your day been?" The words come out stiff and awkward, but still, he doesn't look up. And his thumbs continue to dance without a second thought. He doesn't see that he's killing a part of me.

It's hypocritical to feel hurt by Tatum—to think he's seeing other women. It's just hard to imagine his attention on someone else, especially when he fails so miserably at giving me even the smallest amount of care.

It's cutting close to ten minutes of his thumbs dancing. *Who is on his phone? Why are they so important? Do they know about me? Do they know about us?* I want to ask who it is. I always want to ask. My voice shoots through the air, asking the same question I've asked way too many times lately.

His eyes shoot up at me, burning holes into my skin. There's a hunger for destruction sitting inside of him. I gasp a breath, but not enough for him to notice. "Why do you always assume I'm talking to *someone*?" His voice is sharp and painful. I bite my bottom lip, trying to jolt away the burn of my tears. "I'm writing an email. Is that okay to do?" He stares at me, lips only parted, but I can hear his breath bounce off his lips.

I press my palms together. Tatum's right, I always assume.
Assume the worst. The painful. The heartache.
It shapes my life. Controls. Dominates.

I want to lean in and touch my lips to his, tell him I'm sorry, but I'm unkempt. Nothing will wash away the sin I've just committed.

No, we didn't kiss. No, we didn't touch. August and I sat in a coffee shop and drank coffee together. We spoke, we laughed, we may have even cried. But there was a feeling between us. A feeling I wish was between my husband and I.

My dour mind questions what August would've said if it were him sitting in front of me right now. I want more than *hi* and snarky remarks that make me feel like shit. I want his arms cradling me. I want to feel like me being home makes him happy. I crave urgency for us to touch. That being held back even a moment longer will create havoc in our lives.

It was there during our riotous beginnings. My body used to drown in the thought of his touch. I want him back. I hate this back and forth. I hate that we're on a merry-go-round. And I know sex isn't going to fix all that's wrong but is it bad to want it? Is it wrong to want to be touched by my husband?

"Tatum," my voice cracks. He finally glances up at me, but his emotions are absent. His eyes are vacant and hollow. He brings himself to his feet and steps towards me. It's hard to read what he's thinking.

"How the hell did we get here?" He asks. He moves closer. I don't know what to do or what to say. My arms lay limp. My eyes still bleed. My heart still hurts.

I can't recognize the face I'm staring at—the face I've woken up to the past fifteen years. His arms are lifting. I have no idea what he's doing. Then I realize, he's doing exactly what I wish he did when I walked through the door.

He's hugging me, though it's anything but what I hoped it'd be. He's so far away I can't seem to reach him, even with my arms around his waist. But this is what our marriage has become.

Distance.

Tatum leans back and looks at me.

I look back.

We kiss.

Our clothes come off.

We fuck.

We walk away.

I'm numb.

Everything is dull.

THIRTEEN
Sadie

My hips lean against the kitchen sink with my coffee mug warming my hands. My eyes rest shut and the crisp, morning breeze refreshes my skin from being in bed all night.

Silence hums a song in my ear. It's the only time of day I get to relax. It's the time I enjoy most. It's the best time to focus on what thoughts live inside my head with no one there to deter them.

But this morning, I'm distracted. Tatum left his phone on the kitchen counter last night. And it's soft buzz keeps going off. Part of me doesn't want to look. But the thought of his thumbs dancing—*for months*—gnaws at me without apology. This may be my only chance to see who's on the other end of that phone. I let the thought marinate. *Buzz.* I'm sucker punched by another text. This is my only chance. I have to look. *I need to.*

Alisa: Sorry for texting so early. I'm going to be late to work today.

Part of me is relieved it's only her. Though it yanks on my nerves that she didn't follow company policy—call and leave a message on the office phone. But maybe that's not how he does things anymore.

Another string of annoyance vibrates when I realize how long it's been since I've worked there—realizing how long it's been since Tatum pushed me away. But I walk away from the thought, not wanting to let it sink any deeper.

And I don't dig for more. I don't reach for what's out of sight. I don't try to grab what's not there.

It's Alisa.

It's work.

It's what he's been telling me.

Another buzz stings my ears, but time fails me.

"Good morning," I say to Tatum as he shuffles past me. He groans back with no sensible words. This has become a typical morning for him, grumping and being uninterested.

He grabs his phone off the table. His thumbs dance for the first time today. I swallow the lump in my throat. His phone is more important than saying good morning to his *wife*.

I roll over to see Augusts' face gobbled up from the glow of the morning sun. His faint morning breath lingers on his tongue, but I don't mind it. In truth, I love it. It reminds me that we've yet again made it through another night.

Just like any other day, I wake up to the feeling of his lips pressing against mine. "Good morning, babe," he says. I lean in and burrow my head into his chest. He cuddles me and I fall back to sleep. I don't know what I did to deserve such a love like this. I don't know what I did to deserve him. But I'm lucky.

So, so lucky.

I lean into Tatum, lips puckered, and determined to have a good start to our day. But he turns his head. "Too early," he groans. The coffee pot spits out the rest of his much needed morning fix and hopefully, it'll wake him up.

"Would it be too hard to greet each other in the morning?

Dear Tatum

To start our day off on a good note." He groans, irritated that I've started *nagging* so early today.

It bothers me that we didn't talk last night. I wanted an answer. *What is wrong with us?* Sex has become our new way of communicating. We deal with our problems and our distance by getting closer to one another and stripping our clothes. It's the perfect front—*act as if we care*. It keeps us from saying what we need to say. But who has sex and doesn't kiss? *We do.*

I want to tell him about the speculation happening inside of me. I want to tell him the pictures of him thrusting a faceless woman lives inside of my head. Our love is on its last spark. This is it. There are no more flames after this.

None.

It's always been my duty to get the kids ready for school. And it's never bothered me, at least not until now. Why am I the only one stepping up for our kids? Why does he not seem to care enough? We're supposed to be a team. But lately, we're opposing.

I drop the kids off and race to his office. I'm dizzy from thinking about all the things I need to say. We *need* this conversation. And work is the only place we can't resort to sex.

Gripping the handle to his office, I find myself almost hesitating to walk in. My nerves are tattered because I know this is our last chance to make this right.

I close my eyes and take the step I need. Silence has made its way here, too. Except it's not as gripping as it is at our house. It's calmer here, almost tolerable.

I note that Alisa still isn't here. Not that it should matter to me anymore. This place isn't for me to worry about. It's not where my energy needs to be.

The door to Tatum's office is cracked open. When I pull the door open further, I notice Alisa jump away from Tatum. My posture shifts and my back straightens. No words escape their foul mouths as both pairs of eyes stick to me, wide-eyed and shocked.

The fumes escape through my ears as my stare lingers on

them.

Alisa's eyes dart to Tatum's asking how they're supposed to explain such a scene. But he nods for her to leave. I follow her every move. She's stiff and her shoulders slump forward as she gets closer to me.

"What the hell was that?" I slam the door shut behind her. My hip pops to the side and my hand finds comfort in resting on it.

"Calm down." He mocks me. "We were discussing a patient." I can tell he's lying by the way the corner of his mouth twitches. And if they're up to no good, I will find out. *The truth always comes out.*

I came here to fix what we're doing—how we're living—I need to stick to the plan. We can't afford to get sidetracked. "We need to talk," I say. "About us."

He bows his head and rubs his temples. Harsh air shoots out of his nose. "This couldn't wait until I got home? I have work to do. Patients to see. I don't have time for your insecurities."

I don't have time for your insecurities.

The sad thing about his comment is I'm not surprised by it. He rather continue to circle the game we're playing. He much rather ignore the issues we're facing and continue to let sex be our cover-up. But it's now or never.

I don't care where we are. This needs to be said. "I feel distant from you, Tatum. And this morning despite being in the same room, standing right next to you, I've never felt further away. We've been dancing around each other for years. Maybe you don't want to admit it, but I can't find my husband. He's lost. *Tatum,*" his name whispers off of my tongue. "You stay at work late. You're constantly on your phone. We have sex to run away from the things we're scared to talk about. I love you, but it's time for us to take a step back and realize what we need to fix."

"And what exactly would that be?"

I want to beat him. I calm the scream inside my throat. "I'm not sure. That's why we need to do this together. We need to figure this out, *together.*" He's still for a moment. His thoughts are

Dear Tatum

scouring. I wait patiently to hear what it is he has to say. I hope they're words I can work with, despite how evil or harsh they may be. I just want him to give me something, *anything*.

But there's nothing. His mouth is still hushed. His thoughts are still tearing through him like a monster's claw reaching for his prey. They're hitting him hard. His eyes shut and pinch together. But when he opens his mouth, I'm left with nothing. "I need to go back to work." His phone dings and his attention draws to that.

My stomach hollows. I'm not sure what I was expecting from this, but I thought it would be a good start. I was wrong, *again*. We say nothing more.

I'm nearing Alisa's desk when I feel her eyes digging at the surface of my skin. When she realizes I'm close, she looks down pretending to analyze the papers she's clenching to.

"What were you doing in his office?"

She hesitates to answer. "Looking for new waiting room furniture." Both of her arms wrap around her waist. My sight doesn't waver. It threatens her with the truth. She breaks our eye contact first. She's a terrible liar.

I'm falling into a rabbit hole while climbing back onto the merry-go-round we love to ride. Tatum and Alisa are friends on Facebook. I search the rest of his employees and so far none are friends with him. Nothing else points to anything more than a friendship, but I'm no fool to a cheater. We can't forget I once found it in me to learn how to sneak around.

Confronting Tatum isn't the right move. There's too much room for denial. I need something else. And I'll wait for it because I know it'll come.

Tatum returns home at his normal time. Nothing about his behavior is different. "Hey," he groans, putting all of his work stuff on the floor next to the couch. I ignore his feeble attempt to act like there's nothing wrong.

He notices my eyes haven't left the television, so he comes and sits next to me. His hands lay flat on his lap as he stares in the same direction.

Silence. It's found us again.

It lingers loudly between us.

It stings the pits of our beings.

His phone dings.

His thumbs dance.

We're continuing our merry-go-round.

"About earlier," he says, finally acknowledging there's something that needs to be discussed. "I didn't think it was an appropriate time to discuss our marital issues."

"When exactly would be an appropriate time, Tatum?" I ask. He rolls his eyes. "I won't apologize for coming in. When you're home, you're on your phone and pay no attention to anything else around you." I look over. His face is neither tense nor relaxed. And neither one of us is brave enough to continue to talk.

A continuous flow of what-ifs floods my mind, stirring chaos in my soul. *What if* I chose a different route than the one I thought was my only option? *What if* I revealed my truth? *What if I'm wrong?*

"I know about you and Alisa," I finally say. He reacts quietly, confirming my suspicion. Discomfort befriends him. It's unclear if it's anger, regret, or something other than feeling like what he's done is wrong.

I close my eyes and sink into my breath.

His phone dings.

There go his thumbs, again.

Karma really is a bitch.

"You were never planning for us to renew our vows, were you?" He swallows hard. I assume it's the truth he wants to push down.

But it spits back up. "No."

My head is pounding from the words still trapped in my head. Tatum has nothing to say other than the usual regret package that comes in handy when your spouse is caught cheating.

Take me back.

I'm sorry.
I was lonely.
I love you.
I made a huge mistake.

But I'm not convinced Tatum saw this as a mistake. How many times can you do something and still call it a mistake? When does it become an action? When does it become who you are?

And yet, I feel forced to forgive him. Obligated may be a better word. I dig deep enough to find the truth. I hunt for it, but only to turn around and punish myself. I guess it's the thought of him changing. Watching hot tears burn your wife's cheeks should be enough to change, shouldn't it?

He's asleep next to me. He wanted to have sex to make up for everything, but I turned him down. I can't bear to have another session of exaggerated sex. Fake an orgasm to make him feel good about himself? *No, thank you.*

He's sound asleep. Sleeping as if tonight wasn't filled with strain and trouble. He snores louder than normal. I assume he's thrown a couple back before hitting the hay.

His phone buzzes and curiosity calls. I reach over him, being sure not to disrupt his sleep. Caller ID reads, Alisa. I'm not surprised. I wonder if she knows yet.

Squirming to get out of bed, I answer her call. I give her the opportunity to talk first—to greet who she thinks is on the other end of the phone. "Babe? You there?" Pieces of me fall apart. *Babe.*

"It's not Tatum."

"Sadie?" Her voice shakes, sharing her uneasy feeling. "I'm so sorry,"

"The audacity you have to go behind my back and disrespect me," I say. "You should be fired."

"Sad—"

"No, Alisa. You don't get to talk. Don't ever cross me again. You'll keep your job because I say so. But beware. You are replaceable in every aspect of Tatum's life. Stop calling his phone.

Stop calling him."

Her voice hesitates. She wants to say something, but it claws at her throat. "Can we meet up?" She asks. "Tonight?"

She's lucky The Coffee Bean is open twenty-four hours. And she's lucky that it's the only place I'd step out to at midnight.

I look around and she's not here. I won't be surprised if she flakes. But I'd like to give her the benefit of the doubt. Sitting far enough away from the barista as I can, I wait, impatiently if I'm being honest.

The bell on top of the door rings. There she is. I guess she was brave enough after all. Her cheeks are flushed. Her shoulders are slumped. Her skin is blanched. She looks everywhere but at me.

The chair scratches the surface of the floor. It's louder when this place isn't filled with the sound of other people talking. She hasn't acknowledged me yet. She's hoarding her stare.

Releasing a loud breath, she's realizing I'm running impatient. Her eyes meet mine. They're sunken in and duller than normal. Worry lines her face. She doesn't look as brave as she's acting.

"Tell me everything," I say, demanding the truth. Her head lowers. Soft sniffles slide-out loudly from the small part in her lips. I'm not heating with as much convulsion as I thought I would be. But the longer she sits quiet, the angrier I'm becoming.

I thought of Alisa as a friend. We worked well together. She showed me a lot of promise in her work. We've even gone out after work a few times. So yeah, knowing she's the one Tatum's been dancing for is bullshit.

"I'm sorry," she says. "He told me you were divorced." I gulp. "He told me your marriage has been on the rocks for years." *Well, at least he was honest about one thing.* "And with you not around, his story added up." Her head finds its way back to her lap.

This is why he didn't want me around. It had nothing to do with my dad's passing. It had nothing to do about my healing. He was protecting himself.

This time she shuts her eyes. *I shut mine too.*

Dear Tatum

Tatum knows—*feels*—what's going on between us. And he uses that as an excuse to get women to sleep with him. Half of what he says is true. We're married, but we're barely together. We sleep in the same bed but act as if we're alone. We're apart, yet we're standing right next to each other.

For the first time in our marriage, I flirt with the thought of divorce. I can't see the last spark. Darkness has finally swallowed the rest of the hope we had left. I don't think I have any more energy left to entertain this marriage.

But this means more than divorce. This means coming clean. I'll have to go nose to nose with the dangerous part of me—the part I keep well hidden.

Forgiving Alisa is something that needs to happen. It's not her fault Tatum coerced her into a full fantasy. She's young, naïve and about the same age we were when we first started dating.

I'd assume he filled her with promises that echoed hope and devotion, love, and fulfillment. The same promises he made me.

And despite no foundation under him, I believed his promises. I believed he'd take care of our family. And financially, he does. But physically, he's fallen short of his duties.

A loud cry slips from the grip of Alisa's lips. "I'm so sorry." She cries with her head in her hands. It's sad to watch her unfold in front of me. *This is not easy.* I reach my hands out, hoping she'll find some comfort in that. Her heart burns for different reasons than mine, but she's heartbroken. And that sucks. She didn't sign up for this.

My hands cradle the side of August's face as he's sleeping. I wish to tell him exactly what's going on, but I can't. Fate has reminded me ever so cruelly that it has the utmost power over all of us. No matter what I want, what I do, or what I say, fate will always control us.

Bitter.
Wretched.
Pain.

EMILY REILLY

A river of salt travels down my cheek, surprising my tongue with a burst of an unforgiving taste. August has changed me. He's helped me grow. But admitting that I'm deteriorating from the inside out, that soon I will be nothing, will crush him. I don't know how to say good-bye. I can't and I won't.

I slip into Tatum's office quietly. "Hey," I whisper. He pulls me in and presses his lips against mine, squeezing in his tongue whenever he gets a chance. We both know August can walk in at any moment, part of me wishes he does just to get this over with. Tatum's kiss is neither exotic nor dull, but I can get used to the way it tastes.

His tongue lingers the taste of fresh strawberries. It's refreshing. And I hate to say it, but August's mouth doesn't taste like a fruit medley. Though it doesn't taste bad, it has more of a bitter taste to it. "Sadie," he whispers. "I want to be with you."

"Me too," I wince.

He grabs my hand and places his lips gently against it. "I want my family to be our family. I'm going to take care of you."

I gulp.

"I promise."

The people who say love hurts are right. *Love is complicated.* Love is being vulnerable. Love is being able to un-regrettably share your feelings to progress forward. And exposing every flaw and insecurity and hoping your spouse doesn't use it against you is brave. I expected security, a committed companion. I thought I'd be in sync with my partner.

These are the things we all desire to have and when our expectations fail, heartbreak becomes our new best friend. It's hard to cope. It gets hard to breathe. You try to work on it, but trying too hard is scary. No one wants to look desperate, even in front of their spouse. But when trust is broken, recovering is difficult. This is when love hurts, especially when all you want is everything to work out.

    Fifteen years in the making and Tatum and I still haven't found our ground. We're stuck in the hurt and the pain. It's both of our faults. We're masters at pushing our hurt under the rug. It's been molding our floors for years. But it's about time to get the broom and sweep it out.

FOURTEEN

Harper

Adam's hand slams a single piece of paper down onto the table. It's crumbled and worn. He's standing behind me, trying to scare me into someone I'm not.

See something, say something—and he did. His illusions have surfaced, far and wide. He's taken on the role of my father, even now when I'm forty-seven years old.

He doesn't face me any more. His eyes refuse to touch mine. Maybe he's ashamed. Maybe he's embarrassed by the things he's done. The things he'll continue to do. But no matter the amount of guilt thriving through his veins, he'll still try to punish me in the worst ways. He won't stop until he has the perfect daughter.

His hand is on my chair. His breath is hot and hard on the back of my neck. "I told you you're not allowed to sleep over anyone's house. Not even Brandy." I shake my head. I don't tell him we spent the night on a park bench just to get away from the people who scare us most. "So why did you sneak out last night?" Admitting he's the reason I wanted to leave would be devastating to my own life.

Dear Tatum

I don't want to confront what he's doing—the trap he's putting me in. I don't want the truth to come alive, to burn me even more. I don't want to accidentally admit I'm planning on running away—for good.

—

My brother knows the damage my father caused, yet he still stands proud in the shoes of who he was. He's the only one who knows, the only one who laughs at my pain.

The piece of paper is simple. A doctor's note, forged, of course, explaining how living under my care is unsafe for our mother. My eyes scan the forged document line by line. It twists my past into a list of exaggerated truth to pin me against a wall I don't belong on.

Drugs are a strong part of my past. To talk about it hurts, but it happened. I like to think about how far I've come since then. How my kids are a better part of my life. Adam likes throwing in my face the fact that my mom cared for my kids while I wasn't there. He's twisting that part of my past into now, using that as an excuse to portray my *"inability"* to care for our mom.

It's not something I tell a lot of people. But my brother has a deep need to share scoops of this past life with anyone who'll listen. He needs to see me fail because he can't accept me. He doesn't know how to.

Brandy's eyes switch from me to him. They don't stop. Her foot taps the bottom of the wooden table in front of us. She's watching him maneuver a foreign white powder. "Snort it," he says to me. I stare at the line on the table. She presses her lips together.

I lean forward, but Brandy's voice shoots through the air, paralyzing me. "Don't!" I look up, her eyes are desperate for me to stop. "I don't think you should do it," she whispers. But I don't want to explain to her why I need to distance my mind from reality. I don't want to have to tell her all about what my father does to me. I don't want to admit why I had to run away—why I had no other choice.

"It's fine, Brandy. It's just for fun." The guy next to her pulls her back. He's wearing all black. His arms are filled with scars. I wonder what damages him. I wonder where he wanders too when the sun goes down. Maybe I can go there too.

I snort the line the kid put out for me. My nose tingles, but that's all I feel. "That's it?"

He smirks. "Just give it a minute." His eyes are steady on the line he's prepping now.

I wait a minute and then realize he was right—perfect timing. My lips are being pulled up to a smile, one that finally feels real. I can't feel any of my pain, nothing at all. I'm numb and I like it. I like that my mind isn't scrounging for hope.

"Brandy," I whisper. "You need to try this." Brandy is hurt every day by the people she loves most. Her parents. They discourage her. They yell and scream. They throw their beer cans all over the house and refuse to pick them up. They're toxic. It's why she ran away, too. We're all we got.

She sighs. She knows the dangers, but it's better than our own contorted reality. "Fine," she says. "Just a little." She takes her line and I wait for her shoulders to relax. It doesn't take long.

Before we know it, we're gripping each other's shoulders and spinning as fast as we can. The music's louder. I can hear each instrument playing its part. I can feel each breath I take. I can feel the bones in Brandy's fingers as she grips my shoulders.

I'm aware.
I'm awake.
I'm alive.

"Why did you write this?" I ask. "What are you planning now, Adam?"

"See something, say something. Isn't that what you said?" Yes. That's exactly what I said. I just didn't think he'd go this far. He's an extremist, can't you tell? He gets it from our father.

His blood boils knowing I'd rather be with a woman than a

Dear Tatum

man—knowing I'm the black sheep of the family. I'm the black sheep of most people in this town. He's desperate for me to change, to be someone I'm not. And he'll do anything to shame me for being me.

It's disturbing to think this is better than the truth. *Anything is better than the truth*. Facing those thoughts aren't something I ever plan to do. What my father did—who he was—It's just...*I can't*.

Adam keeps my secret hidden and I don't know why. Thinking about someone other than him knowing is hell for me. Just thinking about their eyes digging small holes into my skin—so many I bleed to death. Knowing this, knowing how much it would hurt me, he still keeps his lips sealed shut. Maybe it's his own reputation he wants to reserve.

"This is going right to elder services," he says. "You'll go to jail for abusing mom and you won't see her or your kids ever again."

All it would take is a single screenshot from Tatum to prove to him I'm someone else. One screenshot. *One*. I can't say it hasn't crossed my mind, but I can't bring myself to do it.

Knowing the truth and knowing how well I care for my mom, I'm still iced over with fear, shivering from the promises he intends to keep. I can't go to jail. Just the thought of going to court, the thought of this town digging into my life—*my past*—haunts me most. "Please," I beg. "What do you want from me?"

"Fuck off, Adam." I turn to see Carson behind us making a cup of coffee. He jumps from his seat surprised she's here.

"This isn't a conversation for you to hear," he says to her. She finally turns around. I gulp and my stomach cramps. She's staring at him as the steam clouds her glasses.

"No one abuses anyone here, so back the fuck off." It's hard to believe Carson would stand up for me. But she's doing it. *Right in front of me*.

"It's fine, Honey. Just go upstairs." Her eyes dart towards me and her brows are angled sharply.

"Don't call me Honey," she says.

FIFTEEN

Harper

My nose has been stuck in my phone more often lately. I've been distant from my own world. The world I belong in. The world I *need* to be in, in order to survive. But Tatum's grasp on me is only getting tighter. His words swallow me whole. I can't slip away.

I don't want to.

Sharpening our feelings from afar is comforting. No one knows who's on the other end of my phone. I can talk to my friends and family and Tatum at the same time. I don't have to answer questions and I don't need to explain who I am.

"Mom," Carson's voice is burning with impatience. "Are you listening to me?" She's asked this question a lot lately. She's fed up with my lack of respect for the value she's trying to share. And the harsh truth is, no, I wasn't listening. Anger swells inside of her veins. It's there regularly, but it's visible now more than ever.

"Hold on," I say, holding a finger up to her. But I walk away. *I walk away from my daughter, willingly.*

Stillness looms between both Tatum and I as we stare at each other through the screen of our phones. He's quiet today—sharing less of what's reeled me in this far. His eyes can't stay still. He's looking everywhere but at me. Lurking inside that head are things he's afraid of—things he doesn't want to challenge.

Sadie is the first villain to pop up. "What'd she do?" I ask. He finally looks at me, but confusion wears his face. "Sadie," I say. "What'd she do now? I can tell you're not yourself."

"She's being her normal, aggravating self today," he says. "But maybe I'm just being a little extra sensitive." I ask what's wrong. Why today of all days is she really setting off a nerve? "I just really like you," he says. I try to center my lips. I don't want to seem too excited and I don't want my smile to linger too long. "But I don't know if you feel the same way." My heart drops. Why would he think that? What did I do to make him think that? My stomach tenses and suddenly I feel like I'm coming down with a fever. "Why haven't you told anyone about us? Like not even your kids."

The tension lessens when I hear where he's headed. But I don't feel good about it. His feelings are ones I've shared more often than I ever wished.

Guilt.

Shame.

Humiliation.

Those aren't fun feelings to play with.

"My kids are too young to understand. What's your excuse?"

"That was harsh," I say. I'm trying not to fall apart. I'm trying not to allow a pit of rage to take over our conversation. He has every right to be angry. I have been hiding him, on purpose.

"I'm just trying to understand, Harper. You vent about how all your life you've never been accepted as a gay woman. But you're with a man now. Now's your chance to wow them."

I steady my breathing and shut my eyes. How do I explain that *wowing* isn't something I want to do? How do I explain myself without making this about me?

"My brother," I say, gulping down the knot burning my throat. My eyes fill with drops of dejection, but I turn the camera to wipe my face. "And my kids, too." He waits for me to continue. "I'm scared."

"Do you always want to wallow in self-pity?"

"It's not that." I snap at him for the first time. Thinking of Adam boasting to his friends about changing who I am makes me sick. I don't want him to think I've changed. I haven't. I'm still me. I'm still the same old Harper.

And the fear of letting my daughters in on my exploration with Tatum fills every crack in my body. Acceptance has never been easy, even for them. Dealing with the opinions of their peers was harder than I thought it would be. And turning around to tell them I'm with a man feels as if everything I've put them through was for no reason at all.

Gloom rides Carson's face. Her shoulders slump forward and she walks slower than she normally does. "What's wrong?" I ask.

"Nothing." Her voice is dormant. The corners of her eyes droop. Something's eating at her.

"Did someone do something?" I ask.

Her teeth grind and her eyes find the floor. "No one did anything," she says. "It's what they said." I tuck my chin into my neck, wondering what it is that got to her. It's hard to imagine the amount of damage to make her this way.

"What?" I ask. "Tell me." Taking a leap, I reach for her hand. I want to be able to comfort my daughter in a time of need, but she pulls away—physically and emotionally. She's always been afraid of getting too close.

"It was Lana." Lana is her best friend. "She said she'd stop being friends with anyone who had a gay mother." My stomach drops to my feet. All of the words I thought I'd say vanish. I haven't come out to Carson yet. I thought she was too young. But it's obvious she knows. I hate that my sexuality is affecting my children.

I hate this.

"I don't know," he says, even after all that. "I'm not a woman, Harper. I'm a man. I can't change who I am."

Dear Tatum

I can't change who I am.
I can't change who I am.

It chants in my head over and over. Its cycle is endless and painful. "And I can't change who I am," I finally say. He can't know what my brother hangs above my head. *He just can't.*

"Just be who you are." His voice softens. "I don't mean to get snippy with you. That's the last thing I want to do. But you're stuffed with judgment. Spill yourself and be happy while you have the chance to." Tatum's serious about us. And I can't hide if I want this to work.

I'm not sure if it's guilt or the truth getting to me, but Tatum's words left a lingering taste of promise on my tongue. No matter who I end up being, I have the right to announce it myself.

Carson's door is the first I open. She's sitting alone on her bed focused on her writing. Noah isn't here today, which always makes her a little colder.

I take a moment to watch how she moves and how effortlessly her fingers glide across her keyboard. This is the only place she shares her unfiltered thoughts. The thoughts she won't tell me. The thoughts she keeps hidden. I wish it were easier for her to confide in me, but I find comfort knowing she found something to help her get through this life.

"Can we talk?" I ask.

"What's up?" She looks up and lowers her glasses. She taps her finger on her lip and I'm aware I'm not welcomed. But I stay anyway.

"What was up with Noah sleeping over the other night?"

"Really, Ma?" she asks.

"It's the rule, Carson. No boys. I don't care how old you are."

"Well, I'm eighteen." *And?* "And the law says once I'm eighteen, I'm a legal adult and can make my own decisions."

"It's my house," I say.

"Yeah," she nods. "It is. But his parents have no problem with me sleeping over there."

105

"Not going to happen," I say. "Nice try. Happened once, won't happen again."

"Either I lie about it or tell you the truth. You choose which one you want." And as harsh as her words are, they're true, because she has no problem going behind my back.

The days of trying to be her parent are slowly ending. I knew this day would come, I just didn't think it would be so soon. I hope there are better days ahead of us. I hope one day we can be friends and look back on the past together. But right now, Carson doesn't want to be my friend. I don't even know if she wants to be my daughter. But I'll never give up trying. It's the least I can give back to her.

"Is this all you wanted to talk about?" She asks.

"No," I sigh. She chews on the inside of her lip, waiting impatiently for me to carry on. I am the biggest annoyance to her life right now. "Can I sit?" I ask, afraid if I do she'll attack, but instead, she just shrugs. "This is going to be weird."

"Just get on with it," she says. "The suspense is killing me." Sarcasm spills from her mouth.

"I've been talking to someone." She sort of rolls her eyes and sighs.

"I've noticed," she says. "Glad you finally moved on from Terra." She looks back down at her laptop.

My voice shakes. "A man," I say. "It's a guy." The words sound awkward and blotchy. Her face turns grave. She brings her thumb to her lips and starts to bite her nail. "And I don't want you to be upset with me."

"Upset? What are you talking about?"

"Well just because of all the things you've had to go through because I was... *gay*."

"I've been through worse." She says it almost as if she's mocking me, which I'm sure she is. "I don't care who you're with, honestly. If you're happy, then that's what matters." I want to ask if she's happy. Does she know what that feels like? *I wonder.* I wonder what it would be like if she smiled more often. I wonder what it would be like if she actually liked me.

She shrugs her shoulders. "It literally doesn't matter," she says. And though her words are short and her face shows me no sign of emotion, they reach me. They're as comforting as she'll allow herself to be with me and I'll take what I can get.

I stand up and walk towards the door. I stop and say thanks before leaving, but she's already immersed in the world she's creating. But that's okay. This was more than I expected.

"Lou," I knock on her bedroom door next.

"Hey mom, come in," she says. "Are you okay?"

"I want to talk to you about something." She gulps and throws her phone to the side, leaning towards me. "I've been seeing someone." She inhales a sharp breath.

"You just got out of a two-year relationship. Don't you think you should take some time for yourself?"

"We broke up a year ago," I say. "And this kind of just sprung up out of nowhere."

"What's her name?"

I look away not wanting to see the expression on her face. "Tatum."

"Her name is Tatum?" Her lip rises with her eyebrow.

"*His* name is Tatum." Her eyes grow wide. I don't say anything more. I just watch her react. Her mind is running out of control. Her head is thrown back and a loud disdainful sigh rushes out of her mouth. I feel like shit. This is exactly what I didn't want either of them to feel, but I get it. I understand the pain that comes with this.

This is really fucking confusing. Seeing me with a man was never a reality in her life. It was never even a thought. But Lou's opinions mean a lot to me. They can sometimes be a deciding factor in what route I choose to lead. We're nearly the same person in the ways we act and react to situations.

After a couple of long, painful minutes of collecting her thoughts, she starts to talk. "What are you doing?" She asks. "Is this something you actually want? Or are you acting out because Terra didn't work out? Or are you trying to impress your Godforsaken brother?" She's pissed. She's *so* pissed. "Who the hell is

Tatum anyway?" Her voice is bitter.

"We connected at my high school reunion," I say. "We've been chatting and he came up here last weekend."

"So that's where you went." She nods, looking away. She falls back on her bed and her chest heaves up and down. Her mind ticks in too many different directions. She asks me to leave and though it's the last thing I want to do, I do it anyway.

I sit in the kitchen and get lost in the empty space in front of me. What the hell am I doing? The night of my reunion I felt this need to live again. I thought Tatum would be that and so far he is. He brings me to life. But am I pursuing him for the right reasons?

Lou storms into the kitchen not too long after me. "Hey," I say. But she rolls her eyes, grabs what she needs, and leaves me to be alone.

"What's wrong with her?" Carson asks as Lou makes her dramatic exit.

"I told her about Tatum," I shrug. "Maybe I shouldn't do this." I take a sip of my water.

"What shouldn't you do?" My mom comes in walker first.

"Going out to dinner with Terra." I look over at Carson who has no intention of backing me up.

"Who's Terra?" My heart sinks. She's met her too many times to count.

My mother's mind has failed her once more. It's a cruel thing to watch. I hate that it's happening right in front of my eyes, and yet, I can't look away. It carries the devil's heart. It doesn't care that it's hurting us—*hurting her*.

"Just a friend," I whisper. "Will you talk to her?" I look back at Carson. I'm begging for her help. She's the only one who can get through to Lou when she's stuck in her own world of thoughts. But Carson doesn't answer. She rolls her eyes and walks away.

My mother and I are left alone facing each other. Her eyes are glued to me and I refuse to look away. A smile sprawls across

Dear Tatum

her face. I smile back knowing that even though she's lost in her own mind, somewhere deep inside is telling her she's happy.

I don't know if telling her about Tatum would be a good idea. Would she even understand? The last thing I want to do is disappoint her or cause her to fixate on something she doesn't need to worry about.

But doesn't she deserve the truth?

"I'm dating a guy." The words bolt out hot and fast. I don't want to cradle the conversation. I don't want to drop hints because I know she won't get them.

She tilts her head and squints. Her mind is going rapid. I'm afraid of the words she's going to say. I brace myself. "That's nice," she says.

That's it? "You're not upset?"

"Upset with what?"

She has no idea.

I get up from my seat. Tears are surfacing. Acceptance comes easy to her now and that should make me happy, but right now, it doesn't. It makes me numb. The thought of anything else is non-existent. I'm dating a guy and that's the end of the thought. Nothing more. Nothing less.

I'm just dating a guy.

Lou makes her way into my room. She's standing in front of me, eyes filled with dire tears. "Is he nice to you?" She asks. I shake my head yes, afraid of my voice shaking. "I'm sorry," she says. "My feelings got in the way of yours. I shouldn't have acted like that." I appreciate her apology. "I just don't want to see you get hurt again. I don't want you to be with a man because you feel like women aren't working for you. Or because someone is making you be someone you're not." She clears her throat. We both know who she's talking about. "I just want you to be who you are. Don't change for the sake of someone else."

"I won't," I promise her.

I won't.

EMILY REILLY

I promise myself, I won't.
I can't.

SIXTEEN
Harper

My thoughts bolster into horror stories. Tension builds. My chest aches and at any moment I'll be dead on the floor from a heart attack. "Breathe," Tatum says. His hand brushes against my thigh. "You shouldn't be the one this nervous." He laughs. "They're your kids." And though he's right, I just can't shake the thought of something going wrong.

Like me, they both carry overbearing opinions. And rightfully so. Their opinions keep my back straight. Their trust has been ruined before—too many times—so if they don't like him it could be fatal to our relationship. Sometimes their eyes see the things I don't. And I'm worried that they'll see something dark in Tatum.

I approach the house, still and stealthily. I press my ear against the door listening for voices. Nothing. *The coast is clear.*

I make it to my bedroom without getting caught. I flick the light on ready to jump into my pajamas, but something damaging is waiting for me. "Shit, Carson!" I yell. She's perched on my bed, staring without swaying. My heart falls to what feels like 100ft. I try not to look in her eyes. I don't want to explain why mine look the way they do. "What the hell are you still doing up?"

"What the hell were you—?"

"Language!"

Red lines of rage swim across her eyes. "I thought she was sober."

"She is," *I lie.* "And so aren't I." *I lie again. She knows I'm lying. And she knows what this means.*

"How can you be with someone who doesn't care about you? About us?"

"She does, Carson." *I start to yell but remember Lou is sleeping in the other room.*

Carson falls apart in front of me. Hurt grows in her eyes. It takes over her light, the one that makes her glow. I grow tense and fall apart with her, only I don't show it.

It's hard to watch her head rest in her hands as she tries to catch her breath. Hugging her would be the right thing to do in this moment. To promise I'll never do it again. To apologize for falling backward. For failing both my daughters. But I can't do any of those things. I don't want to lie, again.

I don't want to hurt her, again.

The two of us wait at the table for the girls. Each second that passes feels like a stretched minute. My foot taps the floor. Tatum squeezes my leg. He looks over at me. A soft smile sits patiently on his face. He doesn't say anything, but I can hear him promise it'll be okay. An urge to kiss him grows in my stomach. *He's perfect.*

Lou's face finally appears. "Hey," she says. "I'm Lou."

"Tatum." He stretches his hand out to shake hers, but instead, she leans in for a hug. She side-eyes me and winks with a smirk.

"Where's Carson?" She asks, getting settled into her seat.

I shrug. "She's coming. *Hopefully.*" We give our drink order while we wait. I have a feeling she's late on purpose.

Dear Tatum

Lou nods towards the door. I turn around and see her walking towards the table. She lifts a hand. I wouldn't call it a wave, but that was her intent.

"Hey." She takes a seat at the end of the table, next to me, furthest from Tatum.

"Carson, this is Tatum. Tatum, this is Carson." My breath shakes as I wait for her to acknowledge him. She's taking her time settling into her seat. It's taking longer than it should. She's avoiding what needs to be done.

"Hi, Carson." Tatum turns his entire body to fully face her.

"Sorry I'm late." Her voice is subdued and her face is blanched. "It's nice to finally meet you," she says.

Tatum and I celebrate by squeezing each other's hands under the table. This is going to be great. I don't know why I was so nervous. *Tatum was right.*

Carson isn't saying much. Lou is doing the talking for both of them. She'll give us a word here and there, but nothing more. And I don't push for more. I can't expect her to open up to him when she won't even open up to me.

A phone rings, interrupting Lou's thought. "I'm so sorry," Tatum says. "This is my daughter." He steps outside for a few minutes.

Lou takes advantage of him being gone. "You know Mom, I wasn't expecting such a wholesome guy. With all the women you've been with I wasn't sure you'd know how to pick a good one." She jokes. A small, sarcastic laugh slithers from Carson's tongue.

"What do you think, Carson?" I ask, not particularly ready to hear what she has to say but needing to get it over with.

She shoves a pile of her food into her mouth. She's reflecting on *something*. "He seems nice," she shrugs. Her eyes venture away from the table.

"You don't mean that," I say.

She drops her fork and looks at me. Misery controls her. "What are you doing with this guy?" She tilts her head to the side and presses her lips into a straight line. I stare, confused, wondering what she see's that I don't. "Seriously," she continues. "I mean come on, Ma. You can't be serious."

"What?" Lou shrugs.

"He's a fucking fraud."

Lou chimes in. Her words are sharp and hot. They're a constant flow of flames. The tension rises between the two of them, but I don't break it up. Instead, I lean back and hope the worst doesn't unfold.

On one side of the table, we have Carson, whose veins are dancing out of her skin. And on the other side, we have Lou, who's ready to claw out each one of those veins. "You come in here fifteen minutes late with a wretched look on your face and you don't even bother giving him a chance." Her eyes bore into Carson demanding an explanation. But Carson doesn't bother. She waits for Lou to finish. "Maybe it's you that's the fraud."

"Really?" Carson climbs back in. "He's sitting here bragging about his business ventures and how much money he has." Her jaw clenches. "You think I'm going to fall for that?"

My fists tighten. My knuckles whiten. I throw down my napkin onto the table. "Never once has he said how much money he has—"

Her voice overpowers mine, trying hard to prove her point. "Oh, he didn't have to," she says. "The way he talks about his fancy cars and his beach house like he's trying to rub it in our face that we live in a middle-class house with Grandma."

Lou makes a face warning me Tatum's coming back. "Everything okay at home?" I ask.

He sits with a smile. "Everything's great. What'd I miss?" My eyes dagger at Carson warning her to keep her mouth shut, which she does, though I'm sure it takes most of her effort. But it's not long until she's running off to work.

Lou stays behind and tries to split the bill. "My treat," Tatum says. "But thank you."

Despite the drama between Carson and Lou, I'm happy they finally met. It was something that was bothering Tatum and the last thing I need is for him to walk away over something so silly.

Dear Tatum

And if it's only the money Carson is worried about, then I'm okay. She'll come around eventually.

"Wanna hit Local?" I ask.

"Totally," he says. "I haven't been there since high school."

"Well, then we have to go." He looks over and smiles. It's hard not to stare at something so perfect. I can't believe how lucky I am. I can't believe it took over thirty years to realize the person I'm supposed to be with is Tatum. *Tatum freakin' Barnes.* If only we knew this in high school. If only *Wren* knew this in high school, she'd kill me.

"Holy shit. It looks exactly the same." His jaw bounces off the floor. I nod and lead him to the boom box. "I can't believe they still have this. This is the exact one, too. Unbelievable." He runs his fingers over the top and the side. I love how excited he is. I love that he can't control himself. I laugh at his disarray.

It's cute.

He's cute.

"What the hell are you doing here?" We turn to see Wren standing behind us. She flips her hair and her hand is on her hip. "So you are fucking her," she says, loud enough for everyone to hear.

My cheeks flush. "It's nice to see you haven't changed," I say. "Great to see you." I go to pull Tatum away, but she moves swiftly, blocking our way out.

"Brandy told me all about the two of you," she says. *Brandy?* "So are you going to tell her or am I?" I look over at Tatum. His back is hunched over and it looks like his lunch is about to come back up.

"Wait. What?" I shake my head. "Brandy told you about me and—"

"Yes. And you know why?" She asks. Tatum stands there with his mouth sewn shut. "Because Tatum and I hooked up the night of the reunion. Promised me we'd get back together and then left me while I was asleep." Her hand is still on her hip. She's mimicking exactly who she was in high school. And I'm trying really hard to stay away from the person I was. Even if it's only to keep me out of jail. "Is that really the kind of man you want to be with, Harper? A man who bounces from woman to woman."

"Tatum," I say. My voice falls flat. "Is this true?"

"I—um," he chokes. "It's not—"

"Yes it is," Wren says. "Everything I've said is true. Tell her Tatum. Tell her the fucking truth! Be truthful for once in your damn life." He looks at her, his eyes infested with hatred.

"All this for what, Wren? To ruin a great night? Yes, Harper's my girlfriend." *Girlfriend?* I haven't heard it out loud before. I like it, I just wish it was under better circumstances. "And yes, Harper." He looks over at me. "Wren and I had sex the night of the reunion. I'm sorry."

I press my lips together and close my eyes.

This can't be happening.

SEVENTEEN
Harper

My bedroom has been my only source of shelter lately. For two weeks I've been avoiding Tatum. For two weeks I've been avoiding Brandy. And Carson. And my mom. And Adam. *Everyone.*

"Mom." I cringe when I hear Lou step into my room. It's nothing personal, but my head is pounding and I don't have the energy to talk. But when I look at her, I don't see the same Lou I'm used to.

"Are you okay?"

"Elder services are downstairs and want to talk to you." *Dammit, Adam.*

"Hi, Ms. Evans." She sticks her hand out to shake mine. And though I don't want to shake it, I do. I have no right to be angry with her. She's just doing her job. "I got an anonymous call worried about your mom." I nod, not surprised. "Who lives here with you?"

"My mom and my two daughters."

"Is there a Noah that stays here, too?" *Noah?*

"That's my daughter's boyfriend," I say. "But no, he doesn't live here. He's slept over a once, but never again." I laugh. She doesn't. "Even if he did, why would that be a problem?"

"It's not," she says. "But we got wind that your mom is being abused," she looks down at the papers in her hand. "Physically and possibly financially? And there are reports here that tell me there's been a couple of falls. Is that right?"

Breathe, Harper. Breathe.

"No," I say. "That's wrong." My throat restricts and tightens my voice. "She's fallen twice because it's hard for her to stand on her own," I pause. "But nobody is getting abused." She marks my words for exactly what they are in case I try to backtrack. But I won't. It's Adam's words she needs to be worried about. "What is going on with this reported financial abuse?" I ask.

"Why don't we talk outside?"

There's an ache that swaddles me and it reminds me I'm alive. The twisting of my pain jabs at my side. The walls that hold me up are crumbling into dust. I'm reaching the edge of disaster. I don't want to see it strike, but it's coming and I can't look away.

My phone rings loud in my ear. It stings. I grow an urge to smash it against the wall. There isn't much more I can take. *Tatum*. The last thing I want to do is argue. But I guess it's better to do it while I'm already down.

"Babe." His voice is edged with concern as if my eyes rimmed with disgrace worry him. "Talk to me," he begs. I try, but the words don't come out. They're stuck in my throat, choking me, taking away my right to breathe. "I'm sorry, Harper. For not telling you the truth." He thinks my tears are for him. And part of them are, but I don't have the heart to tell him what's *really* wrong.

"I don't want to be hurt anymore," I cry. "I'm so tired of being hurt."

"I'm coming up there," he says. "I'm booking my flight now. I need to fix this." His concern is comforting. For once he's not latching with excuses, but with solution. Admitting he was wrong is big for him.

I'm learning Tatum's faults. Some are harder to look past,

but overall, I can see through him. I can see the better side of him clearly. I choose to look in the better direction, *the promising side of him.*

Tatum's back is towards mine, pouring himself a glass of wine. My eyes rest on the movement of his body. He rocks with ease and edge.

I sneak up behind him and wrap my arms around his stomach. I'm happy to be here with him. I'm happy he decided to come see me—*to fix things*. Even though I'm sure this visit was more because he has work to get done for the convention than needing to fix things face to face. But I enjoy it for what it is.

He laughs, softly, and squeezes my hands. He turns around and we're now facing each other. "I'm sorry," he says again. "I didn't know I was going to fall in love with you."

"You're in love with me?"

"Of course I am," he says. "What happened with Wren—" his voice fades out. "I was horny." I laugh and shake my head. Not really because I find it funny, but kind of. "How was I supposed to know I'd see you at that party? I didn't know my life was going to change."

"I guess I just thought you hated her."

"When you haven't been laid in a year, or two," he laughs. "You take what you can get." Fair enough. "Have you talked to Brandy?" I shake my head no. I don't know when I'll talk to her. I don't know if I want to. "I don't want to lose you over something that meant nothing to me." His bloodshot eyes stare into mine. He pulls me in closer and I bite my bottom lip craving his taste.

His lips find mine, and the taste of promise bathes on his tongue and crawls into my mouth. It's sweet like the wine he's drinking. He pulls away for a moment and lets his eyes do the talking. He leads me to the couch and lays me down. He handles me as if I'm a piece of glass that's easily shattered. Part of that is true. But this?

This won't shatter me.

He crawls on top of me, but he feels so far away. Gripping his shirt, I pull him closer.

Our tongues dance.

Our hips grind.

I want him so bad.

It's been over twenty years since I've been with a man this way. It feels like being deflowered all over again. The same racing heartbeat slams against my chest. The same gut feeling of *oh shit, this is happening*, sits in my stomach.

"Are you sure this is what you want?" He asks.

I answer by kissing him harder, deeper. Pressing my body into his, I dream of the moment both of our clothes are off, but it doesn't take long.

My eyes are kept on him as he peels each layer off of his body. Every moment, every movement brands my mind. My breath grows heavier when the last layer is ripped off of his skin. *Oh my.* I gasp. *It's my turn.* But instead of me peeling off my own clothes, he reaches for the bottom of my shirt and takes it off for me. He bites his lip before unclipping my bra.

I surprise myself when I notice I'm not hiding my stomach. The scars that stain my body should be one's I'm proud of. Two pregnancies gave me these stripes, but they damper my self-confidence. But comfort comes naturally around him and I'll take that as a sign of doing the right thing.

This is not a mistake.

My underwear is off now and my body is exposed and open for him to judge. He leads me from the couch to the bed and climbs on top of me.

I close my eyes and breathe.

"Are you ready?" He asks. I nod. This is exactly what I want.

I grip the sheets and my knuckles turn white. My legs fall to the side, allowing him into a space only a few are able to get too. *A sacred place.*

"I love you," he whispers. I pinch my eyelids shut and let his words dress me with feeling. We haven't said those words directly, but I think they're true.

I love him, too.

EIGHTEEN
Harper

Adam's boots hit the floor behind me. I'm not in the mood for his shit today. "Hey Ma," he says as he walks into the kitchen. I roll my eyes. His voice goes right through me. My mom turns around to see who it is.

"Adam, is that you?" She asks.

He leans down and gives her a kiss, then turns to me. "I heard you got a visit the other day."

Moving my eyes from my phone screen to him, I let out a hot breath of air. "Yeah, I did."

"Any thoughts?"

"Mom, we'll be right back. Lou's upstairs if you need her." I lead the way to the porch. Not only would our mom not understand what's happening, but rallying her confusion only adds unwanted stress to her mind. "How could you do this to me, Adam?"

"You live a life of sin and I don't think that's healthy for Mom."

"So you're trying to kick me out?" He shrugs. "And what the fuck is this?" I throw the stack of papers the woman gave me. *Supposed evidence* of me stealing her money.

"You tell me, Harper," he says. "Why are there so many checks written out to you?"

"There are these things called bills that are due every month. I'm not sure if you have any, but here in this house, we do. And I can't afford all of them on my own."

"So that includes paying for Noah's housing too, right?" He asks.

"Noah doesn't live here, Adam. I don't know where you get your information from but it's not accurate."

"I saw him here the day mom fell," he says. "He slept over and don't act like that was the only time." Of course, Adam is here the *only* day Noah has ever slept over and now I'm paying the consequences. "So yeah, I really think you should find somewhere else to live," he says.

"And who do you expect to take care of Ma?"

"We'll hire nurses."

"We?" I ask.

He nods.

"No," I say. "We won't. Because I've looked into how much they are and let me tell you something you don't know. You need a lot of money to hire a nurse to be with her all of the time. *A lot of money, Adam*. Do you have a lot of money to spend on her? Are you willing to spend thousands of dollars a month on your mother?" For once, his lips are sewn shut. "Are you going to sacrifice your time for her? Are you going to have your kids help her? Make her lunch? Make her bed? Help her in the bathroom?"

His chest heaves up and down. His temper is starting to kick in. His eyes are narrow slits that carve out chunks of my skin. And yet, he says nothing. Slamming the door behind him, he leaves. And for now, I take it as a victory, at least until the next battle begins.

"So what? Noah isn't allowed to come over anymore?" Carson asks.

My lungs deflate and I close my eyes, so I don't accidentally take my anger out on her. "Enough with the bullshit, okay? No one said your boyfriend can't come over anymore."

"It was just a question." She spits the words out like her tongue is a knife. She's always trying to cut me. *Always*.

I don't know what to do. How can I move away from my mom who needs me the most? I can't do that to her. No matter what happened between us, she needs me now.

But Adam's destructive agenda could ruin how everyone looks at me. He can take my life away with just a couple of words. He's taking bigger steps and eventually, I'm going to run out of energy.

"Harper!" I turn around and see Brandy standing at the front of the cereal aisle. I almost turn around and ignore her. *Almost*. "I've been calling you."

"I know," I say. "I haven't wanted to talk." She tries to grab my hand, but I pull away. "How could you do that to me?" I ask. "The day you were late and told me you ran into her. That's what she told you, isn't it?" She's quiet. "Why wouldn't you tell me?"

"I—Harper," she stutters. "I'm sorry. It was a one-time thing and I thought you and Tatum would be cute together. And all the drama that happened between you and Wren, I didn't want it to deter you."

"Well it would've been nice to know the truth," I say, nodding my head. "And then lying about Tatum wanting to call me?" I shrug. Her lack of being able to tongue the truth bottles me into frustration.

She tugs on my arm. "Please, Harper. I'm sorry. And I'm sorry I lied about the number thing. But the way he described it, I thought it'd be worth you trying it out." She says it as if it's her decision to make. "I just want you to be happy." And as much as I don't want to forgive her, her intentions were thoughtful and kindhearted.

"You better not be hiding anything else from me."

"I promise," she says. "There's nothing else."

The obsession to heed the truth can be damaging, especially when you have no evidence of a lie. Can your gut actually detect when something's off? Or is it the scars that bleed your past that obscure your pleasure?

The distance between Tatum and I is starting to trickle in. It's creeping up in the worst ways. My mind is being told his truth is fabricated. It's being hammered with false nothings that I turn into something.

"Remind me again what you did last night?" Tatum sighs at my lousy attempt to find a hitch in his story.

"I can't keep going over this with you, Harper. You either believe me or you don't." It's not that I don't want to believe him, I do. But I can't seem to shake this uneasy feeling piercing my only sense of logic. It's difficult to wrap myself in his words. Something feels...*missing*.

But he's glued himself to this story and doesn't waver a detail. He hangs up, sick of the back and forth, and my thoughts begin to twist even more of his story. I'm beginning to think that's my problem. I'm digging for an issue that isn't here, allowing my insecurities to reel me in. I'm trying to convince myself this is wrong when it's not.

"What are we having for dinner tonight?"

My jaw clamps shut. "I don't know, Carson. Fend for yourself for once." My tone is sharp. I watch her face tense. Her eyebrows knit together and she walks away mumbling under her breath. My head falls to my hands ashamed I let the anger I'm holding in for Tatum out on her.

Fault finds me and fills me with self-disgust. I'm harassing him to find truth in my insecurities. Who does that? I stare at myself on the screen waiting for him to answer my call. Each line that carves my face reminds me of all the shit that's made me this way.

The ring never ends.

I throw the phone to the side of my bed and sink into my pillow. Time dissolves into nothing as I wait for his call. I find myself tapping the screen of my phone every two minutes hoping

Dear Tatum

Tatum appears, but he never does.

I should apologize to Carson, too. And though my apology to Tatum seems more important, Carson's is the one scaring me most. We aren't a family that coddles our problems and throws them out to be fixed. We hide behind them. We sweep them under any rug we can find and leave them there as long as we can. *We leave them to rot.* My parents taught this trait well.

Brandy's nose is covered in our favorite white powder. I laugh while taking another line. I hate to love this feeling. We're loose. We're far away from where we started.

"Whatever happened between you and Wren?" She asks, wiping the tip of her nose. I don't know if sharing the details is something I want to do right now. It's a lane that brings me downhill. It's a lane that's forced me here. "You know you can tell me." I know. She prepares another line and waits for me to answer.

The door creaks open. Damn it*. I try to clear the room as fast as I can before getting caught. "What the hell are you two doing?" Adam steps into the room. We try to explain, but his voice outweighs ours.*

*"No. No. No. No. Adam, please," I beg. "Don't tell Mom." My hands are folded together. "*Don't tell Dad*." The corner of his lip rises. Sin sings from his pores. He enjoys the torture. And if he wonders why I've let myself go, this is why.*

His throat opens and the house is scorched by his voice. The patter of my mom's feet rushes up the stairs. Her breathing is heavy. All I can do is stand still, forcing my heels into the ground.

My hand holds my head in place, afraid of meeting the disappointment in her eyes. I can't bear the humility swallowing her up. Brandy stands behind me as if somehow I can be a shield to what's going to happen next. "Don't tell your father," she says.

Don't tell your father.
So much for trying to help me.
So much for trying to figure out why I'm hurting.

Carson's an emotional hoarder, keeping everything that shapes her vulnerability hidden and stored away. I've taught her that. I taught her to hide and to be scared and closed off.

"I'm sorry." Carson looks up from her computer. Her fingers stop moving. They stop her mind from flowing, from letting out what she needs to hide.

Her blue eyes have fallen gray from the hurt she stashes away. I wonder what that is. What hurts her the most? Is it me? Am I the root of the pain and discomfort that drives her? Is her misery simply a reflection of how she feels about me?

"All good." Her voice is short and un-amused. Her eyes shoot back to her laptop as if I'm no longer here. But I don't want to let this moment slide away from us—*from me.*

"How's your writing coming?"

She shrugs. "Just like any other day," she says. "Hard to focus." And that's my cue to leave.

Why is my ceiling so dusty? *I should clean that.* It's crazy, really, how gravity is constantly trying to pull it down, yet it finds the strength to hang there. *Despite the burn.*

I want to be as strong as that dust on my ceiling.

Strong.

Resilient.

Stable.

My butt vibrates and I leap across my bed to see Tatum on the screen of my phone. "I'm sorry," I say before he has the chance to tell me how wrong I am. "It's hard to see what's real and what's not when my—"

"Stop," he says. I pull my shirt over my mouth. Here comes the *I'm sorry, but I can't do this anymore.* I brace for the familiar feeling of heartache about to creep in. It's made a nest in the center of my chest for easier access.

Tension builds between my teeth as I clamp down my jaw. I don't want to hear what he has to say. "I am so in love with you, Harper." He gulps down more words I'm not sure I want to hear and I'm glad he doesn't let them out. "But I don't know if we can

Dear Tatum

work through this distance anymore. It's too much."

I whisper his name and start to cry. I'm crying real tears for him to see. *I hate this.* I hate that he can see my pain. I hate that he can how much he really means to me.

"I can't move back to Washington. I have kids here. I have a business. It won't work."

"So that's it?" I shrug. "We're just done? No looking back?"

Lines form around his eyes. Wrinkles that weren't there before have made an appearance. "No, Harper. I can't lose you. And I'm pretty sure you miss me when I'm away." I do miss him. I always miss him. "I want you to move in with me. I want to start a real life with you, Harper. I want to wake up and be able to kiss you. I want to hold you in the morning. I want you to be mine every single day."

I press my lips together. He makes me feel like a light in the darkest room. I love the way he makes me feel. He's the only one to make me feel like I deserve a spot in this life.

But moving away from my family isn't something I can do. It doesn't matter if I'm ready or if I'm not. Being away from my mom, away from my kids—how would that look?

Adam wouldn't let my mom leave. No way. And Carson? She has a life here with her boyfriend. Lou has a great job and finds comfort here at home. To give that up? *For me?*

"Tell Carson if she wants to come, I'll match her pay. She can be my office manager. And if Lou decides she wants to come, I'll find a spot for her too. And there's plenty of room for your mom. And hey," he says. "The warm weather might be better for her." He finds good reasons for them to tag along. I just hope they're enough to get them down there.

"Absolutely fucking not," Carson snaps. "There's no way in hell I'm moving down there. Not today, not ever. I don't need his job offer." Her voice is grim. "You know, Ma, I'm actually disappointed you even asked me. The fact that you'd assume I'd leave my life here, leave my boyfriend, for what? To play happily ever after with *your* boyfriend? You don't even know if you'll be with him in a year."

"Why would you think that?" I ask.

"Do you want me to pretend that I don't hear the two of you arguing almost every night on the phone?" She shakes her head. "You're still as selfish as you used to be." She storms away before I can say anything back.

My eyes fall shut before turning to Lou. Her face is long, shaking her head no. "I'm sorry, mom," she says. "I can't leave Grandma. You know Adam won't take care of her." I've never wished more than right now that Adam would step up and take responsibility, and stop hurting the people around him to get back at me.

I refuse to leave my family behind—*not again.* Carson's right. It was selfish to assume they'd follow and leave their lives behind. I don't know how Tatum's going to take it.

I don't know if we'll survive.

I don't know if... I'll survive.

NINETEEN
Harper

I'm shattered with the thought of losing Tatum. It's like two ropes are pulling each of my hands in the opposite direction. Carson hasn't looked at me since and Tatum's convinced I'll leave no matter what.

"Noah," I yell in a whisper, catching him alone. "Is Carson still mad at me?" He shrugs. That means she is. He just doesn't want to say it. "Can you just talk to her? Tell her I'm sorry."

The corners of his eyes sag a little more than usual. "I don't know Harper," he says. "Maybe she'll change her mind."

Maybe she'll change her mind?

Leavenworth doesn't have a lot to offer me. I'm stuck living between the past and what will come next. The fear of what Adam will do next pushes me into the ground. I'm worn out and tired. I don't want to fight for my freedom forever.

My mom sits in her usual spot in the kitchen. Next to the window and in direct sight of the birdbath she put up years ago. She stares out at it and watches the water fly out as each bird comes to bathe. She watches life come and go.

Her limbs don't move nearly as well as they did before. They're stiff. They've been stiff for a long time. I wonder what it feels like now that her mind is slipping. What does it feel like for your brain to *stiffen*? To watch life continue to thrive...

The thought taunts me.

Confusion glazes over her eyes as she stares at me with a face that doesn't look familiar anymore. Even if Adam let me take her, pulling her away from a space that comforts her will only worsen her condition. She needs familiarity and consistency.

What I'm about to do almost shatters me completely. Risking her health for Tatum—is he really that important to me? Yes, he is. He's everything I need.

Everything.

The question scorches flames throughout the kitchen. I'm burning away the longer I wait for an answer. This is my only chance. And for a moment it almost seems like she's taking it into consideration. Almost like her mind is working how it used too.

My mother's face is stolid—eyebrows knitted together into a straight line. "This is what's going to happen." Her voice is grave. Closing my eyes, I inhale a sharp breath before she continues. "You won't tell anyone about that bruise and I'll talk to your father." Her eyes penetrate the surface of my skin, dimming the lights with the strength of her stare. "But you need to keep your sexual fantasies to yourself. And you will never do that again. Understood?"

I nod, though I don't want to.

This is not a fantasy, Mom. It's who I am.

"I've lived here for over fifty years, Harper," she sighs. "I'm not leaving." The words flow out too easily. Maybe I'm the one who's lost my mind. Despite knowing that was going to be the answer, I still decided to ask. I decided to set myself up for failure. Who does that?

"I can't come," I say when he answers my call. I don't look at

Dear Tatum

him. I can't. Seeing the disappointment would only echo the hurt.

"Is it really that important they come with you?"

Excuse me? I finally look over at him. I can't read what's written on his face. Is it hurt? Anger? Disappointment? Either way, that's my family.

"And you're letting them hold you back," he says. "Like you always do." *Like you always do.* "You can finally escape Adam."

Escape? He says that like it's easy. Far or near, he has information that can hurt me and he knows it. Far or near, he'll find a way to damage me. He'll continue ripping me apart just like my father.

"We can't live like this forever, Harper."

The thoughts pawing my mind are starting to bruise. I can't stomach the thought of leaving either side behind. It almost feels like he's making me choose, them or him. *He doesn't get it.*

So many memories come to mind. Ones that make me want to stay and those that make me want to flee. I was born into a life I never asked for. But I have a real chance with Tatum—a chance to make something of myself, even if that's just a wife. *He wants me.* Tatum really, *really* wants me. That's not something I've felt before.

I don't have time to lose him.

I don't have the time to make another mistake.

My shadow follows me even in the darkest places. It's glued to my back whispering the promise of explosion. I don't want to be here for that. Leavenworth is dangerous. *Adam is dangerous.*

How can I stay here?

Carson walks into the kitchen. There's something different about her. Her already sad eyes look even sadder today. Her already slouched shoulders, slouch even further. Her hair sits on top of her head in a knot, something she never does.

I almost ask what's wrong. *Almost.* The thought of annoying her more scares me away. I'm poked with pain watching her aura turn dull. A mother shouldn't be scared to comfort her daughter. *But I am.*

A knot crowds my throat. The need to understand her weighs heavier with each passing day. There's pressure to understand the anger that's made a home in her.

She grabs a mug. A mug that isn't *her mug*. It's weird that she's making coffee in the middle of the day. That's not part of her routine. Her mouth is sewn shut. All that's present is the sound of coffee spitting from the Keurig.

She pours the sugar. Her eyes, bonded to the steam floating above her cup, stare into a place that's not here. The pour hasn't stopped.

"Carson," I say, snapping her out of whatever was playing inside of her head.

"Damn it." Her tongue is sharp. Whipping the mug into the sink, she pours out the fix she needed.

"Are you okay?" I ask.

"I'm fine." Her eyes don't reach me. Her tongue's still sharp. There's a shake to her voice. Something's digging at her. *Something's destroying her.* She doesn't bother making another cup of coffee.

"What's wrong with her?" Lou asks.

"I was just going to ask you the same thing." I hate this circle we live in. We're all so afraid of speaking about what drowns us at night. Constantly living in fear of opening ourselves up—afraid of being vulnerable.

Knock, knock.

"What?" Carson yells from the other side of the door. "Just come in if you want to talk." The handle of her door is cold. Her room is dark. The last place she needs to live in is a dungeon. They're toxic places. No light lives there. No life thrives there.

Admitting I'm nervous is an understatement. But I need to go in. I need to be her mother for once. Her curtains are drawn so light can't make it in. It's just as I pictured. Clothes are thrown on the floor. Her bed is a disaster. A single lump pops up from her bed. She's hiding.

But from what?

Dear Tatum

"Wanted to know if you needed anything." A rough silence builds between us.

"I'm fine." Her voice shakes as if speaking to me is the worst thing that could be happening to her right now.

"No, you're not." I take another step in and close the door enough for only a strip of light to shine in.

Heavy gasps creep from the corners of her mouth. She's drowning in her own tears. Crying in front of me is killing a part of her right now. *It's killing a part of me.*

The limbs on my body melt away. I'm turned into nothing. She won't even look at me. I was selfish. If I knew asking to move would hurt her so much, I never would've risked it. I guess Noah couldn't get through to her.

I'm sorry. The words linger in the air, echoing inside my head. She needs to hear the words from me. And it doesn't matter how close I am to Carson, she's always ten steps further away. So, I take another step.

And another.

And another.

My shins graze the side of her bed as my heart beats through my chest. It knocks me off balance. Tiny bits of sweat swim through the lines in the palms of my hands. I take another step and lie down next to her.

We lay still, trapped between these four dark walls. I move my hand to the top of her thigh. I want her to tell me what's drowning her, but the words are having trouble surfacing.

I fucked up.

One too many times.

Marvin's hand has a fist full of my hair. He's screaming. A 'v' forms on his forehead from the veins that pop out. The kids are crying in the corner, but he doesn't seem to care. His rage is more important right now. He pins me against the wall, not caring both of our daughters are watching his every move.

"Please stop," I beg. He blinks as if he's snapping out the fit of

rage he's in. He lets go of my hair and steps back. He shakes his head and swallows a large gulp of saliva.

This is the first time he's gone this far. His eyes droop. He's ashamed of what he's just done. I don't blame him for being angry with me. We're not in love. We're not who we're supposed to be.

I need to leave. I can't face my daughter's small eyes staring at me wondering why I've let him do what he's done—like I'm weak.

I am weak.

It's been a month since I've been home. The kids are at my parents. I've been on a roller coaster. I hate this feeling. I hate the rush this white powder makes me fall in love with. It rips me apart, yet promises healing.

I need to go home.
I need to get help.

I left when my daughters needed me. I can't leave Carson again. Not now. *Not when she needs me most.* I press the palm of my hand on her back. Her chest heaves up and down, too fast for her to catch. "What's wrong, Carson? I'm sorry—"

"Noah broke up with me last night." My heart drops. I want to pry. I want her to tell me what happened. I want her to trust me enough to open up, but she won't.

Her pain unfolds right in front of me. I can't help this. Heartache is a pain you have to experience. It's inevitable and hurts the most when you least expect it. And even though pain is one of my closest friends, not even I've managed to slip away from him.

I feel useless.

Again, I place my hand on her back hoping it'll help her find some comfort, even if it's just finding her breath. But it doesn't help. I take a moment to do something I never thought I'd do. I wrap my arm around her and pull her into me. She cries. *Harder.* Tears fall and make a mess of my hand. But I pull her in even

Dear Tatum

closer. I'm holding onto this moment as long as I can.
I'll hold onto her as long as I can.

Life after heartbreak is undeniably cold. Carson's head hangs lower than it normally does. Her words are shorter than normal and no one dares to step into the place she keeps hidden from us.

Distance is nursing us again. Holes scorch through the limbs in which we need to talk. It's as if we're forbidden from talking about the night we got too close.

I almost got my daughter back that night. I had her in the palm of my hand. Resting between us was the ignorance of the past—as if it never existed—as if all along we were a unit.

Sustaining an appetite when you're aching with loss is near impossible. I'm trying to be her mother—still. I had her for one night, no thanks to the tragedy burrowing inside of her.

"Do you think they'll get back together?" Lou asks.

"I don't know."

"Will who get back together?"

"Grammy," Lou sighs. "I told you three times already. Noah broke up with Carson."

"You didn't tell me that. Is she okay?"

Lou's eyes dart towards me. The corners of her lips fall into the place no one wants to visit. "She'll be fine," I say, hoping it's true.

"Can we talk?" Carson stands in the doorway. The brims of her eyes are rusted. Patting the bed next to me, she comes and sits down. "Are you still planning on moving?" I almost bolted out the word no, but I stop myself because I don't have a solid answer yet.

"I haven't thought about it much lately, why?"

Her head tilts to the side and her sight floats away. "If you do, I'll go with you." I don't know what to say or how to react. Smiling wouldn't be appropriate, but turning her down doesn't seem to be the right thing to do, either.

"What about your work?"

"Screw work. I'll take Tatum's offer." Her hands fall into her lap. What kind of mother would I be to thrive off of my daughter's heartbreak? "I can't stay here anymore, Ma."

"Running away isn't the answer though." Her face is washed with discomfort.

"I'm not running away." Her voice sharpens. "I'm moving on. I can't cry about No—" She stops. She can't even say his name out loud. "I just need to move on." Neither one of us says anything more. And I'm left alone to sit with the thought of what this means for us. Do we run away? Or do we continue to drown in Leavenworth and hope that somehow we make it out alive?

She's asking to be brought into the life I share with Tatum. And it's not that I don't want her there. Believe me, I do. But even though she's asking for this, I don't think it's something she actually wants. Carson shouldn't be somewhere she doesn't belong simply because she feels like home isn't home anymore. That's not what she deserves. *It's not what anyone deserves.*

"You have mail here," Lou says.

"Just leave it. I need food first," I laugh.

My mom's brittle fingers struggle to open a pack of pretzels. "Ugh," she groans.

"Let me help you," I grab the pretzels out of her hand and open them for her.

Her eyes meet mine, and the light on her face dims. "What's wrong?" The look on her face...*her eyes*...they're lifeless. Her shoulders are in her ears. Her mouth ajar, just enough to get some air in. "Mom," I say. "It's me, Harper." She hears my name and only then does my face become familiar.

"I know it's you," she says, sticking her nose in the air. But the truth holds strong in her eyes. There's no denying what was lost in that moment.

Knowledge.
Familiarity.
Understanding.

Dear Tatum

I've never seen my mom as mad as she is now. It's been five days since I've seen her face. It's been five days since she's seen mine. It's boiling red, instead of the pasty, flesh color it normally is. "Where did you go?" I don't tell her. "Where did you go?" Her voice gets louder, harsher. I haven't seen this side of her before, the side she hides.

The dark side.
But still, I say nothing.
I can't tell her why I left. I can't tell her that my brother told our father behind her back. I can't tell her what he'd do to me. I can't tell her anything.
She doesn't understand.
She leans on the kitchen counter and throws her head back. A harsh breath shoots out of her nose. The anger she's feeling isn't something that's just surfaced. It's been there for a while. It's been brewing—boiling.
This isn't her.
I close my eyes when I hear her step towards me. I don't know what's going to happen, and I don't want to know. "I'm going to ask you one more time. Where the hell did you go?" Five days I was gone. Five days I bounced from one park bench to another. Five days I ate food anyone would spare me. Five days I spent thriving off of my beloved white powder. But my lips are sealed. Her hand wines up. She's taking part in my father's game.
My face burns.
My heart burns.
My life burns.

Her hands move slower than they used to. She can't slap me now. She can't punish me. I need to move on. Move on from always being the disappointing daughter. Move on from the thought of my mother loving me for exactly who I am.

I need to move on.

She picks apart her sandwich, taking off the top layer of bread. She pokes it and moves it around her plate. Her lips tighten and her nose scrunches. A rush of air shoots out of her nose and she stands, abruptly.

"What's wrong?" I ask.

Her hands take ahold of her walker as if they knew they belonged there. "I need a fork."

"It's a sandwich, Ma. Just use your fingers." I piece it back together the best I can. "Here. Take a bite." And she does.

It's hard not to wonder if she'd do the same for me. *Probably not.* But watching isn't an option. Suffering isn't an option. I can't be the one to let her down.

A sandwich. That's all it took to make up my mind. A sandwich was the defining moment in my decision. Who would have thought?

My phone rests in my hand. I know what I have to do. I type the words out. *I'm sorry, Tatum.* Cowering in fear of his response, I continue to write. *It's not going to work.* The blue arrow that sits next to my message laughs. It laughs at the truth. It laughs because it knows how much this hurts, but without delay, it will send him the message I don't want to say.

"You okay?" My stomach plummets when I look up and see Lou gnawing on a sandwich. She uses almost no effort to shove the two slices of bread into her mouth. Eating a sandwich shouldn't be hard, but for my mom... *it is.*

TWENTY
Harper

Lou's eyes are sharp. Disappointment and shame live there. Lips sealed shut, yet I know exactly what she wants to say. I shake my head back and forth, "I can't."

"You have too," she says. "I love you mom, but Adam isn't going to stop. There's something seriously wrong with him. And we don't have the means to fight his battles in court." She shrugs. "I can take care of Grammy and I will."

"I can't ask that of you." I say.

"You're not." She picks at the side of her finger. "You deserve this."

"Deserve what?"

"*Freedom.*"

Fear wraps its sticky fingers around my throat and tears me in different directions. Running away from Adam will confirm I'm still the same person I used to be.

Sore.

Powerless.

Crushed.

Carson stands in the doorway of my room. "Can we talk?" I motion for her to come in. Quiet and frail, her eyes drift away.

They're so afraid of meeting mine. They always have been. "We shouldn't stay here," she says. "There's nothing here for us."

"That's not true." My voice drops and suddenly I'm defending this place like I believe in it—like somehow overnight it became the only place we belong. "We have Grammy and Lou. You have your friends and a great job."

Lines etch above her eyebrows. "And what else?" She asks. "Because all I see is a lot of bad shit that neither one of us wants to live with anymore." And she doesn't even know the half of it. "Whether you and Tatum are together or not," I hate when she says that. It rips me apart. Tatum and I may not be perfect, but he makes me feel like I am. "I don't think Leavenworth is for us anymore. I know it's not for me anyway."

Her words absorb into me, but it's not enough to change my mind. Pointing to the door, her eyes follow my finger and she sees what I'm trying to say. She looks back at me and hollows into nothing.

Adam's heavy footsteps creak against the wooden floor, and I don't need to see him to know he's behind me. "Heard you're thinking of moving."

My heart sinks and it's as if his words rip away all of the air I need in order to stay alive. "What are you talking about?" I ask.

"Stop playing games, Harper. You're not going anywhere." His breath pants on the back of my neck, making the hairs stand up. I stand to my feet and he almost falls to the floor.

"Leave me alone, Adam." Turning to leave, his voice murmurs something I wasn't prepared to hear.

"But I am glad after all these years you finally figured it out." I almost turn around. I almost growl back. *Almost.* But I'm not starting another war. *Not now.*

Brandy's drink slams the counter hard enough for it to spill. "What happened now?" She asks, slurping off the drops of her

Dear Tatum

drink from her hand.

"He knows about Tatum." Her back stiffens into a slight curve.

Teeth gritted together she asks, "Do you know who told him?"

I shake my head. Her hands tremble as she squirms in her seat. "Are you okay?" She gulps a big sip of her vodka tonic before looking at me. Her eyes are stuffed with something I'm not sure I want to know. They stare at me hard, and the more I look back at them, the easier it is to see the regret living there.

No...It can't be.
But how?
Why? "You can't be serious?" I ask.

Her shoulders collapse and she cries out the words, "I'm sorry. We ran into each other the other night at the bar down the street."

"How could you do that to me, Brandy?"

Her voice cracks and she tries to grab my arm, but I yank myself away and stand up. "I'm so sorry. Please, Harper. Don't go. I was drunk and mad at him for treating you the way he does." I can barely look at her without seeing the sheer panic that covers her. She doesn't want to lose me, she just got me back, but I think it might already be too late.

Digging into my bag, I grab my cash and throw down enough money to cover my part of the bill. I don't bother looking back at her. I keep my focus on the steps I take, hoping the humility doesn't knock me off balance.

I guess it doesn't matter how old you get, people are always going to backstab you, and cry when you feel it come through the front of your chest. They'll apologize because they *"didn't mean it"*.

I don't think anyone means to be an asshole, they just are. Brandy's shell fell open today. I saw her for who she really is. She knows how Adam treats me. I guess I just thought she understood.

I melt hearing Tatum's voice when he answers the phone.

It's everything I need right now. "How's Brandy doing?" He asks, but I shake my head and look away. "What happened?" I've never told Tatum in so much detail about how my brother treats me, but it feels right to do it now.

He shakes his head and tightens his lip. He's beside himself, feeling hurt by what Brandy did. I've never seen the ugly live so bright in his eyes. His anger touches me with comfort. It's hard not to like the way he defends me. "Why are you smiling?" he asks.

I shrug. "I just… I like that you care so much."

"Of course I do. I love you," he says. "Why do you think I want you to move into my house?" The rage has settled some, but it leaves a coating behind, reminding me how much he really cares. My shoulders fall forward as if the weight of his words hit me from that back. I haven't told him my definitive answer. I never pressed send. I'm regretting it now. Big time. Because now we both have to hear the words that want to destroy us. The ones we don't want to hear out loud. At least, I don't anyway.

I wish I could have mastered the art of putting my feelings into words. Every time I talk it feels like no one can understand what I'm trying to say. Things come out and feel open-ended. It gives people the opportunity to reel me back into a small space. And when it comes to this, I don't want to sound open-ended. "I can't move," I say, hoping my words are blunt and to the point.

"But Carson's looking forward to this," he says.

"This isn't about Carson," I tell him. "This is about me and my life."

"All you do is complain about your life, Harper. I'm giving you the chance to start over in a new place. I'm doing that. Me. For you. Everything I do is for you." His voice grows louder and the coating of rage sitting on his face is turning on Brandy and falling for me. "And you're going to do that to me?" He falls quiet for a moment, and I swallow what he's just said. Everything he does is for me. *Everything.* I've never heard those words before.

"Well at least you still need to come up to prep for the convention," I say, hoping that'll ease some of the pain.

"Yeah, well, that's not going to be forever. The convention is only a year away."

"So we have a year to think about it." I shrug.

"That's not going to work for me." He looks away from his phone. There's a silence lingering between us, cramming us into a small, and suffocating bubble. "What about my mom, Tatum?"

"What about me?" He asks. "What am I supposed to do? We need to be together. We need to live under one roof. If I didn't need this I wouldn't be inviting you to move into my house." He says it like it's something I don't want for us. But how many times can I tell him now isn't a good time. When will it make sense to him?

"Then we can't be together anymore." *There it is.* "Living so far away from you? I-I just can't do that. It's not enough for me."

"Tatum," I cry. "It's not that I don't want to. I just can't. Not right now. Not with my mom like this."

"Lou can handle her. She's not as bad as you're making it out to be."

"Excuse me?" My voice sharpens. "She can't even eat a fucking sandwich."

"Lou can take care of her, Harper," he says again, settling his voice. "You're giving up your life, again. Why?" He asks. "Please tell me why. After all that she and your father put you through. It's not fair to you. It's not fair to us. *It's not fair to me.*"

"I can't take away my daughter's freedom," I say. "I've been a pretty shitty mom in the past and I don't want to be her again." My voice shakes admitting a truth I'm so afraid of reliving. And sharing my vulnerability with him always feels like a loose screw, like it has to be there but needs to be tightened.

"Babe," he whispers. "You're a great mother. And your mom has a lot of time left in her. Don't focus on what she can't do because it stops you from seeing all the things she can." He does have a point. I focus too much on what's wrong, rather than what's right.

Lou bursts through my bedroom door yelling. "The cops are here." I sink into my bed before rushing down the stairs to see a police officer standing in my living room. I guess Lou was right, Adam isn't going to stop.

"Hi, Ms. Evans," he says.

"What can I help you with, officer?"

"I'd like to talk to your mom for a moment." I lead him into the kitchen—the space where my mom likes to sit. Where she can watch the birds. Where life thrives and she can smile watching it. I think her favorite part about watching the birds fly by the window is that she understands what they are, and I think that's what makes her so happy.

"Hi Mrs. Evans, how are you?"

"Oh. Hi," she says with a panic to her voice. *Thanks, Adam. Thanks for scaring Ma.* "I'd like to talk to you for a minute if you have some time." He sits in the chair next to hers and starts to talk. He pokes jokes and laughs with her as if she's of sound mind. He's the only one to talk to her like she's an adult nowadays like she can pick up on social cues, sarcasm, and jokes. I like that he's treating her like a human, and not a vegetable. He looks at me and suddenly he's not joking anymore. "I'd like to talk to her alone."

My foot pounds the floor as I eavesdrop from the living room. Lou sits across from me, her eyes wide and stuffed with concern. "Did you actually take money from her?" She yells in a whisper.

"What? No, of course not. How dare you even question that?"

"Then why the hell is he saying there's proof of this?"

"You know as much as I do."

"Your son is worried about you, Mrs. Evans. Are you sure you feel safe here?"

"Adam," she washes his name away with a groan. "Him and Harper have always had issues," she says. "Harper takes good care of me. She wouldn't do that."

"Are you sure? Because we have documents showing there are checks written out to her from your account."

"I signed them," she says. "She pays my part of the bills with that money." And for a split moment, my mom is back, but this time she's defending me.

My mom is defending me.
Like she actually cares.

There's nothing left for him to say. She's said it all. She's said everything I needed to hear. *Absolutely everything.* "Ma," I say. "I'm sorry for what Adam's doing. I wasn't going to tell you we were having issues."

"Well, the truth always finds a way to reveal itself, Harper." I guess Tatum was right. She has more of her mind than I presume she does.

I deserve Tatum. I deserve to have him close to me, to hold me, to kiss me good morning. *I deserve that.* And none of us here deserve Adam's antics. The stress he lays on this family hurts all of us, not just me. And without me here, he won't be able to hurt my family anymore, *just me.*

"Lou," I say.

"Yeah, mom? Come in."

"If I were to go—" My tongue tries to squish the words I need to say away, but I try to be stronger than the pull. "If Carson and I decided to move, you'd take care of Grammy?"

"Of course," she says. She doesn't hesitate.

"But if she gets worse you need to tell me. You need to tell me when it gets to be too much."

She nods.

"Please," I say. "Promise me."

"I promise."

TWENTY-ONE
Sadie

Tatum and I have taken an unconventional twist in our marriage. We're moving forward with our lives, *together*. But the cycle ends here. This time for good. We both need a step back to reclaim our love for one another and assure it's still there for us to feel.

Tatum's apartment is only five minutes away and I miss him. But not coming home to him feels—*good*. Better than I thought. And the secrecy hiding in between these walls left with him. The air flows better now, like finally I can breathe in my own house.

There's a banging on my front door interrupting the calm that's nesting itself here. But I sink into my couch instead of looking to see who it is. I lay still in case whoever it is tries to peak in. But instead, they make a distasteful move and jiggle the doorknob. I jump to my feet and my eyes bounce from spot to spot to find a weapon I can defend myself with, but I'm left empty-handed. Just as I'm about to bolt, Tatum's face appears from behind the door. "Jesus, Tatum! What the hell are you doing? Knock next time will you?"

"I did. And you didn't answer." He obviously doesn't know

how to take a hint. "Mind if I come in?" It would be senseless telling him no when both feet are already inside. "How've you been?" It's been almost two weeks since I've seen him. Seeing him knocking on our door is weird. But I guess you can say it's not actually *our* door anymore.

It's almost impossible not to note the shift in energy the moment he's inside. "I wanted to give you these," he says, handing me a dozen pink roses and lunch from my favorite sub shop. My lips curl into a sheepish smile. "How are things since I've left?" He asks. He's torn between sitting and standing, making himself comfortable or being in a hurry. He can't read me and that scares the hell out of him.

He's aged since the last time I've seen him. New stripes of gray hair stagger his head. Bags live under his eyes. He's even been touched by lines crossing his face.

It frightens me that I have little to no care about how he's feeling or what he's going through. It's the first time I've found myself empty when it comes to his feelings. "Everything's great," I say, breaking eye contact. The urge to keep moving is consuming me. If I don't focus on putting these flowers in a vase, the words I shouldn't say may catch up to me. I'll hurt him. I may even hurt myself.

He senses the tension steaming off of me. He makes an effort by walking over and coddling me with a hug I don't need. Squirming in his arms, I manage to pull away, reaching for my cup of coffee.

My name spills of his tongue, making my body quiver in the worst way. "I miss you." He tries reaching for me again, but I manage to slip away—*again*.

Despite what he's done, he's still human. He still has feelings and I need to carefully tell him mine without stabbing him where it hurts most. Talking is problematic for us. He's emotional and sensitive and takes everything too personal. I've dimed my emotions to save his for too long. My feelings matter too.

His words whisper in my ear, leaving a trail of things I've been trying to run away from. It makes my head spin in every direction. I slam my hands on the counter and close my eyes. "I know you miss me, Tatum. You've called me every day since you've left, leaving me voice mails, emails, and texts. I'm tired of it. I like not having you around right now. You moving out was because we needed space. You're hovering and I'm suffocating."

My eyes, dark and empty, meet his. His eyes swell with emotions he needs to sort through on his own. My words sound cruel, but they're honest. At some point in my life, I need to start being honest again.

Living in a world where love overpowers all and nothing comes in between us isn't realistic. It's a fantasy. It always has been and I've lived in there for too long.

"I'm hurt, Tatum. My heart hurts. My body throbs just looking at you. My bones are frail and flakey. You hurt me so bad," I cry. "I need time to be alone."

He glues his eyes to the floor. "I'm sorry," he hums. "I really screwed up."

"Well, sometimes sorry means nothing," I say. My past experiences carved this into me.

I dig my face into my pillow trying to suffocate and kill the pain inside of me. Yet, August floats in and ruins everything I want to fix. He always finds a way to creep into my head at the worst times. He sits there and lingers, pestering my thoughts of Tatum.

Past sparks ignite. They pain pieces of me I've tried so hard to let go of. Everything about August is a constant reminder of what my life could've been—*what it was.*

My lungs feel empty.

I'm running out of air.

I'm running out of air.

Help.

A throbbing pain in my head wakes me up out of the sleep I want to stay in. *9:30pm.* I blink to adjust my sight to the black hole I'm living in. The rims of my eyes are swollen and puffy, and it feels like I have bags hanging from my lashes.

Dear Tatum

There's a deafening silence stinging my ears. It burns through the house. I assume Tatum took the kids to his apartment.

It's lonely, again.

I'm lonely, *again*.

The stairs creak with each step I take. The T.V. is on and the noise only adds to my headache. He couldn't have shut it off before he left? *Ugh*. I almost fall onto my back when I see Tatum sitting on the couch. Only his eyes move. They meet mine.

I don't panic.

I don't run away.

His lips press together before saying the words, "I'm not giving up on us."

"Where are the kids?" I ask, ignoring what he said, but absorbing every inch of it.

"Sleeping." He stands to his feet, taking one step towards me. Pieces of his face fall into the shadows of the T.V. "I'm going to show you just how serious I am about making this work." I stand limp, processing his words.

He's trying.

Now, it's my turn.

TWENTY-TWO
Harper

Every part of me aches with a smile. Knowing that in a short few months I'll be waking up to the man I love everyday buries a new piece of fulfillment inside of me. Tatum loves me and that's all I've ever wanted. I've always wanted someone to hold me like I'm theirs—someone who'll see all of my scars and will still decide to dance with me.

Tatum sees through my scars.

Today, I walk into work with a smile. I'm giving my notice. I'm finally leaving. I'm leaving this office and this town. I'm leaving the past, so I can finally have a future.

I've found a way to center myself and blur the chaos that comes with my decision. Nothing can steal this feeling. And if all else fails, I have Tatum by my side and that's the only thing that matters.

TWENTY-THREE
Sadie

I'm blinded by the morning sun. Squinting, I see drips of drool drop from Tatum's mouth. I laugh and then do something neither one of us has done in way too long. I press my lips to his and finally, it feels just right.

A soft laugh that sounds more like a moan escapes when I feel him kiss me back. His hand finds the back of my head and caresses it. With ease, he tosses me on my back and slips off his boxers. All without breaking our kiss.

His cold hands trace the length of my legs promising me our time has just arrived. It almost feels as if someone has plugged me into him. We're connected in the strangest, most beautiful way. And for the first time, I'm not thinking of the woman he's done this to behind my back.

Both of us are naked now. Our breaths are growing shorter and feel heavy on each other's skin. We roll through the sheets effortlessly. Our skin melts when touching each other, feeling like we're one.

Wanting more of him, I press my body deeper into his. My fists clench the sheets and my neck rolls back. Soft moans come from each of us. I'm ready to finish. *So close.* I am so close. It's been fifteen years and this is the first time I'm not faking it.

"I love you," I say, meaning it. A smile peaks from the corner of his lips. He whispers the same words back, this time without hesitation. The three words I once found difficult to find are sitting right in front of me. They're holding me.

Our spark didn't go out. It's light merely fell flat. It's been waiting for the perfect moment to brighten again. And this was it. This was our perfect moment.

"I'll drive the kids to school today," he says while brushing the hair out of my face. I almost lose my breath knowing he *chose* to drive the kids to school.

I go to the only place reputable enough to celebrate our progression. Standing in line, I fester on trying something new. I've been drinking the same drink for over twenty years. And while I carry out an entire debate in my head, I don't even realize it's my turn.

"You're up," the person from behind me says. Laughing at myself, I step up to the counter.

"Your usual?" The barista asks.

And instead of my normal *yes*, I say, "today I'm going with something different."

The sides of his lips widen with his eyes. "Wow, Sadie. I'm shocked," he says. "Is that all for now?" We laugh knowing this is only the first stop of the day.

"No," a voice from behind me shouts. "I'll take an iced regular, cream, and sugar please." I look behind me to find August handing the barista his card. Staring at the smile on his face, our world feels flipped upside down.

"You don't have to do that," I say.

He shrugs with a smile. "Here are your drinks." Staring into the eyes of August, I regret my impromptu decision to torture my tongue with this unfamiliar taste. But I'm not sure if it's because it's gross or if it's August's perfectly shaped, almond eyes smiling at me.

Buying me a drink obligates me into inviting him to sit with me, even though that's the last thing I want to do. Tatum and I just started to get our groove back. Risking that by indulging in August sounds like disaster. But I ask anyway and of course, he says yes.

"How are things with Tatum?" He asks. I fall back in my seat taken aback by his sudden interest in him. I can feel myself falling down a rabbit hole. What do I say? How do I say it? Should I be honest? Do I tell him we're living apart or lie and say we are living our happily ever after?

The one we were supposed to live.

"Things are…" I inhale a long breath. "Okay," I say. I'm downplaying our morning, but I have to remind myself this is only day one. Tatum still has a lot of catching up to do.

"That doesn't sound convincing." His voice is stern, but not unnerving. I hate how much I love to look at him. I hate that he knows me better than Tatum.

His power to understand me is terrifying. It's something Tatum's never been able to achieve as my husband. When Tatum looks at me, it's as if he sees through me. But, August? *He sees me.* Even after all these years.

Tatum skims the surface of my world, while August digs into my words. He looks for the things I don't say, but want too. And he swims down even when it gets hard to hold his breath.

August lays his hands out in front of me, but they're not trying to reach me. They're resting. And without thinking, I rest my hands on his. I almost regret it by the way his chest heaved up and down, but without a second thought, he intertwines his fingers with mine.

Complicated feelings funnel in the pit of my stomach. The pain of hurting him lingers around me. My actions were cruel. No matter how he feels—*how I feel*—what I did is unforgivable.

I do not love him.

I left him for a reason.

I do not love him.

I left him for Tatum.

"I'm so sorry," I say, pulling my hands away and letting them fall to my side.

I don't look up, but I can feel his eyes on me. They're sticky and hot, burning me with guilt and regret. "Why do we always end up here?" He asks. My lips press together holding back the words I *really* want to say, but never will. They hold back the truth—the answer he needs to know. "I wish we didn't—"

"No, you wish I didn't do what I did," I blurt out. "But I did, August and you have to move on." It's my fault. I'm the one to blame. Yet, I push my anger onto him as if he deserves it.

"I loved you," he says. "I still love you." My shoulders ache forward, wishing I could say the same words back. How can I? Tatum's finally trying. *I'm finally trying.* I can't let that go. "Please," August cries, this time reaching for my hands.

"Please don't do this to me," I say. I close my eyes, afraid of meeting his—afraid of what they'll tell me. His words are broken. It's hard to believe after the damage I caused he still loves me. I don't deserve him. I've *never* deserved him. "What exactly would you like me to do, August?"

"Leave him," he says. "There's no way you're happy." *No way?* How the hell would he know?

"Do you even remember what I did to you?" He squirms in his seat as if his past hurt is flashing through his memory. I hope this changes his mind. I hope he runs away and never comes back. His lips seem to seal themselves and everything I've ever felt drops to the floor.

I can't listen to the fantasy living in his mind. Our truth is dark. Together we're dark. We've formed a fantasy that will live forever in the shadows of what could've been.

I walk away and focus on each step I take, trying not to fall. There's an uncomfortable pit in my stomach holding me in a place of discomfort. The air is becoming stale and hot. Beads of sweat drip down my back. I'm rushing to the door, but gripping the handle doesn't help settle this feeling.

I don't bother looking back to see if August is following me. I hope he's not. I need this moment alone. Safety comes when I'm inside my car. All of my emotions pour out of me as if the damn I've been trying to salvage has finally broken. My tears burn my cheeks, leaving what I hide for everyone to see.

My oxygen is disappearing, escaping my car and leaving me with nothing to inhale. The gray sky is too bright. Black dots blur my vision. I'm disappearing and I'm letting it happen.

The last thing I ever wanted was to be a woman who jumps back and forth. Judgment is worse than being ripped apart by the devil's accomplice. Silent judging will haunt you no matter where you go. Their words invade your mind and stay there like demons that have attached themselves to you.

I jump when I hear banging on my window. August's eyes are narrowed into me as if they're trying to reel in a part of my soul. I don't throw a fit or start a scene. I roll my window down, but neither one of us can find the right words to say. We know this is finally the end.

He sweeps away the piece of hair that's fallen into my face, then leans in and kisses my cheek. I hate that I loved that.

"August," I cry. "I can't do this."

"I know." His voice is soft. "I want you to know that I love you. And no matter what happens between us," he pauses. "You're always going to be the one I want, Sadie." I want to wrap my arms around his back and fall into him, and I want him to hold me like he's never letting go.

I almost let the eight-letter phrase roll off my tongue, but I stop before it's out. No more words are spoken. An awkward smile plants across his face. It's neither happy nor sad. It's more of a confused, please come home kind of smile.

I'm left watching him walk away—the same view I tortured myself with years ago. His shoulders slouch forward, wishing the outcome were different. I wish it were different too, but our lives are what they are.

My heart shatters.
Good-bye August.

TWENTY-FOUR
Harper

Tatum and I have been cutting the edge of what seems to be a constant downward spiral. His eyes have been heavier lately. They don't look at me the same way. And I'm not sure if it's because he's nervous or stressed about the move. Maybe both. But he seems less excited than he was.

I stare at him through the screen of my phone. His eyes sit far away from mine as we sit in this awkward, uncomfortable silence. There's a harsh truth sitting on the edge of his tongue waiting to hit me.

"You can't move in with me." His words jab a sharp pain in my stomach

"You're joking, right?" I ask.

He nods his head no.

"But we move in two weeks," my voice shakes. He sits quietly, eyes meeting mine in the worst way. It feels like life is disappearing in front of my eyes and stripping me bare. I understand now why he's been so quiet.

Offering bad news is never stress-free. Getting the words out will claw at your throat, but now isn't the time for him to quiet his voice. He can't leave me alone sitting in the dark. "You begged me to move in with you. This wasn't for me. This was for us." *For us to be together.*

His voice wraps around my words and strangles them with every ounce of anger he has left. "Sadie doesn't know about us!" He yells. "And all her shit is still in my house," he says it as if it's my fault. His words leave me feeling empty. It's as if he's stripped me of all the things he's been filling me with. "I thought everything would be figured out by now," he says, rubbing his head. "It's just not a good time to come down here."

My fingers curl into hard fists, turning my knuckles white. This isn't something we decided yesterday. We've had months. He's had *months* to get this done.

My anger continues to sit in the palm of my fists. And I'm glad he's not with me right now because there's no saying what I'd do. He screams and yells and tears his throat apart and refusing to say much back only angers him more.

The longer I stay quiet the more I wonder what the hell is going on. What's gotten into him? *This isn't Tatum.* It can't be. This isn't the man I fell in love with. He doesn't scream like this. He doesn't allow rage to consume him like this.

"I left my job," I say. "I've told everyone I'm leaving. Including Adam. What do you expect me to do? Live on the streets? Stay here?" He closes his eyes, and I can see the worry sitting on his face.

"It would be unfair for you to move into a house filled with Sadie's things," he says in a much softer voice. "I still want you to come." His words throw me off. That's not what he wanted five minutes ago. Did he forget he said this was the wrong time to move? *The wrong time.* "You can move into my summer house. It's only an hour away."

"Only an hour?" He shrugs as if that's the best he can do. "Did you forget I still have to commute to work every day?"

"It won't be for long," he says. "I promise. Its just Sadie is—" His voice fades out. "I don't know what she'll do to you and Carson if she finds out we're together. And if she comes to get her stuff and you're there..." He shakes his head. I don't look at him because, despite the anger braiding me, I can understand where he's coming from, but it still hurts. "Assure me you're still coming," he begs. "Please."

"Assure me that my daughter and I have a place to sleep at night if we still do."

His voice gets loud again. He's shaming me for thinking he'd leave me to the streets. "You deserve more than that," he says. And I hope he's right because after this week I don't have a job anymore. I've already been replaced.

It's scary to think he didn't think this through—to make this a priority. *He lied to me.* He promised me a home, *with him.* But I guess it's different when you're not the one uprooting your life.

I put off telling Carson for now. I can already feel the resentment pouring off of her. Tatum's thrown me for a loop. I rush to the toilet and the little food that's in me manages to surface.

Closing my eyes, I can feel my bed sway back and forth. *Is Sadie really that crazy?* Or is our relationship a fantasy? I don't have the answer. And that's one of the reasons I don't want to tell Carson. She's going to bring up questions I hadn't thought about but should've. She's going to want to know why Tatum's playing with our lives and I don't want to bear witness to the knives in my back—*the ones Tatum has left there.*

"Are you okay?" Carson catches me alone in the kitchen. Her eyes point at me as if they know what's going on inside of my head. I bite my lip, paranoid she overheard our conversation.

"We aren't moving into Tatum's," I say. Her movement stops. She stands still, but tense. There's a burning silence standing between us. It's loud. It's screaming. "We're moving into his beach house instead," I say trying to make it sound more appealing than it is.

"Why?" Her voice is stern. I hate the look in her eyes. It's the look of disappointment. It's a look that makes me feel less of a mother.

I gulp down the nerves holding me back from telling her the truth and everything spills out. I try to excuse what he's done as if he's a hero who fell into our lives. But I should've known she

Dear Tatum

wouldn't fall for it. She lives too far away from fantasy to fall into a hole of mischief.

"I thought they've been divorced for months." She stands with her arms crossed around her chest.

"They have been," I say, jumping to his defense.

"And you believe him?" I did…until she asked. Living twelve hundred miles away from each other makes it easy to hide things you don't want to be seen. "Do you?" She asks again. My mind was so loud I almost forgot Carson was standing in front of me.

"I-I don't know." She's planted a bug in my head; one that feels like a tick that's already had too much to drink.

"Then you need to figure it out. You're not just playing with your life anymore. You're playing with mine and I don't appreciate this bullshit."

"But it's not my fault."

"Yes, it is your fault." Her voice gets louder. "You're an adult, Harper!" *Harper?* "You should've planned better than this. We aren't moving down the street. Don't you get that?" Her words sting even the strongest parts of me. I can't afford to lose Carson, especially over this. I need the answers. *I need the truth.*

My eyes are red and weary from the LED light that's been blinding me for the last two hours. I drag my eyes across the screen and search high and low. I go wherever the Internet takes me. And it tells me everything I need to know. It gives me the answer to Carson's question.

I barge through her bedroom door, eager to give her an answer. "Yes, I say. "I believe him," I make myself comfortable on the end of her bed. "He's telling me the truth."

She doesn't look up. She stares at the words she's spreading across the screen. "And you know this how?" She asks.

"I looked Sadie up on Facebook and there's nothing on there. Well not since him and I have been together."

"And you think because you didn't see any pictures of them online, he's telling the truth?" Her eyes finally meet mine.

"I mean, yeah," I shrug. "People put their entire life on there."

"Not if they're trying to hide shit," she says.

"Sadie wouldn't know he's trying to hide. So if she wanted to post about them, she would." And if Carson doesn't want to believe it, then she doesn't have to. But he's telling the truth. He loves me too much to lie to me. And I feel horrible I even questioned his loyalty. If the worst thing we need to do is stay in a beach house for a couple of weeks, I'll take it.

As long as I'm with him.

TWENTY-FIVE
Harper

Today is the day Leavenworth stands behind us. Carson's eyes have been swollen since yesterday, yet I haven't seen her cry once. She's breathing the heartache. I understand the hurt because no matter how much I can't breathe in this town, leaving it behind is hard. But leaving will allow us a better life—one we've deserved for so long.

I wish I could take away Carson's pain, but I can't. And it's not that I wish heartache on my own daughter, but she needs to feel this. There's no potion to dissipate hurt. You can only deal with it. Ram it into the ground. Jump on it. Push it. But you can't run away from it. *You need to survive it.*

An unhinged feeling lingers in the pit of my stomach as we merge onto the highway. Carson isn't much of a talker, but I'm hoping this will help open her up. We have a twenty-four-hour drive ahead of us. Can she really sit quiet the entire time?

"Does Noah know you're moving?"

She rolls her eyes. "Really?" She asks. "I don't talk to Noah anymore."

She's hiding from her feelings again. I don't blame her. I'm hiding from mine too, even though it's the worst thing we can do.

One day it's going to catch up to us, and when it does it's going to hurt like hell.

There's a lot of tension between Tatum and I right now. And it's selfish to not let Carson in on it, but I don't want her to stress about things that aren't meant for her to worry about.

Deep down I'm happy. I'm glad I took this step. Because even though Tatum and I aren't living our greatest moment, this is the start of our life together and we have forever to make it right.

TWENTY-SIX
Sadie

Isn't Disney World supposed to be the happiest place on earth? Because right now it feels like the opposite. The kids are in the back seat cheering when they see the sign welcoming us in. Tatum's thumbs have been dancing the entire way here, promising me they'll stop the moment we arrive. But I have a hard time believing it.

Breathe. Focus on what's good. That's how we'll get through this. We walk towards the entrance, both kids holding onto my hands. Tatum's thumbs stopped dancing—*for now*, but his phone sits in the grip of his hand drowning in the desire to look at the screen.

It's hard not to notice how low his smile sags and how the crow's feet droop around his eyes. I thought you got crows feet from smiling too much, yet he rarely does that, at least around me anyway.

No matter how many times he tries to convince me, this is the last place he wants to be. I try to pretend I don't notice. And I'm not sure how good that is for our marriage, but if it means our kids will have a good day, then I'll do it.

"Can you take our picture?" I ask a woman standing by. We

stand in front of the iconic entrance, the one with the castle behind us. Forcing Tatum next to me, I pull his arm around my waist. "At least pretend you like me," I say joking around, but meaning it.

I hope our good moods last, but I can feel them ending before our adventure even starts. Tatum's energy is heavy and is weighing me down. His thumbs will dance soon, toiling with my emotions.

"Can you at least pretend you want to be here?" I ask, whispering for him to get off his phone.

Hot air shoots out of his nose. "Not that you would understand, but having your own business requires me to be available at all times. Just enjoy the day. Stop looking for a problem."

A knot ties in my spine, building pressure that needs to be released. But I squeeze my fists and remember today is for the kids, not for us.

Tatum lags behind and I'm trying not to care too much. He's the one who will have to live with the consequences of being a father that always stood too far away.

"Hey, wait up!" He yells. My shoulders relax when I hear the urgency in his voice. Finally, he's ready to be with his family.

"Hi, Daddy," Charlotte says.

"Thanks for joining us," I say, trying not to fake a smile.

"I'm sorry," he says. "I actually have to go. There's a work emergency."

"No way." I start to laugh, thinking there's no way he'd leave us at Disney World.

But as always, I'm wrong. "Wish I was," he says, kissing both kids and leaves us behind as if we don't mean anything, as if today wasn't meant for us to all be together.

Tatum stumbles through the door an hour and a half after he was supposed to be home. My eyes stagger to him and a novel starts to fester.

He looks like he wants to say something, but doesn't know

how to say it. What do you say to your wife after leaving her and your kids in Disney with no ride home? How does one work their way out of that?

"I'm sorry," he says.

These are the things that stunt our growth. These are the things that make me regret my decisions. It's clear we haven't jumped out of the cycle.

We're still circling.

We're still dancing.

We're still hurting.

"Babe," he whispers. He wraps his arms around me. I refuse to melt into him, no matter how badly I want too. Giving him the satisfaction of hurting me—*the kids*—and coming back to only say I'm sorry, won't cut it.

"If we're going to work on this then I'm not going to hold back the shit I need to say. What you did was beyond fucked up." He nods his head agreeing with me. "And even when you were there, you barely spoke to us. Do you really think I'm not going to ask for your attention?"

He hugs me tighter, keeping his lips sealed shut.

"I'm serious," I say. I pull out of his grip, meeting his eyes. Their feeble attempt to look like they're hurting makes me sick to my stomach. *He makes me sick to my stomach*.

His hair sits out of place. His clothes are ruffled. He doesn't look how he should. "Why the hell does it look like you just got done fucking someone?" There's an urge to tear him apart—physically and emotionally—but I close my eyes and breathe my way through it.

He stutters. *A lot*. I cross my arms waiting for his explanation. "Was it Alisa? Did you somehow convince her this time we actually got a divorce?"

"No," he shouts. His cheeks are flushed and he tries to defend himself. But his words feel chaotic and loose. Ironically, his phone goes off mid-sentence. And without hesitation, he digs into his pocket as if we aren't discussing something crucial to our marriage.

His thumbs dance.

His mind disappears.

And I'm left all alone.

"So who is it?" I'm no longer afraid of his reactions. They give me the truth even when his words don't. He doesn't pay mind to my question, but I'm not allowing him to slip away that easily anymore. "I'd be careful if I were you," I say. "Because this game you're playing is getting old really fast." His eyes shoot up and pierce mine, yet he has nothing to say.

My phone rings and I look down to see August's phone number flashing across my screen. My heart drops. I almost want to hide it, but don't want Tatum to notice.

Guilt swallows me back up and I'm back to drowning in the shadows of my own faults. I ignore his call, but a text follows.

CALL ME NOW!!!!! Wileys hurt!

Tatum leaves the room. He has nothing more to say and I have better things to worry about. "What happened?" I ask in a panic.

"Car crash." My heart drops. She told me her plans to see her jailed brother-in-law. I told her not to go. I told her the coward wasn't worth it.

Being here with Tatum, working on a failed marriage is the least of my worries now. "I'm leaving," I say. "Wiley was hurt in an accident." Tatum jumps to his feet as if he actually cares.

"Is she okay?" I shake my head afraid if I use my voice I'll start to cry. I can't cry in front of him. He doesn't deserve to see me at my worst. I'm losing my husband and I might just lose my best friend.

TWENTY-SEVEN
Sadie

Wiley's head leans to the side. As of now, the tubes coming out of her are her only reason for survival. Cradling her hand, I can't help but feel a tiny bit blessed I can be here for her, even in the worst of circumstances.

For once it's me holding her hand.

It's uncomfortable hearing the doctors say they don't know if she'll make it. We spoke yesterday. She was okay. She was fine. And she was breathing on her own. I promised her the hardest days are gone, that the storm will be over soon, but promises mean nothing if tomorrow's fate is already made up.

Wiley can die any minute. Her heartbeat can fail her. Time can fail her. The thought of her fate already being determined is unnerving.

We're never guaranteed tomorrow. I've always known this, but right now...*it's come true*. Living as if there is a tomorrow is foolish and I can't live like I'm always going to have one.

I only have so much time left and I need to use it wisely. Time waits for no one, and it won't wait for me. I can't promise myself one day I'll be happy with Tatum. I'm not happy with him now. And I don't think I ever will be.

TWENTY-EIGHT

Harper

We're so close I can almost taste Tatum. Picturing our life together has seemed so far away, but now? Now I'm three hours away from it.

I'm not sure what this life is going to bring me. I don't know what I'm going to face, what kind of mazes I'll have to run through or how many dark ally ways I'll have to search. But I'll be with Tatum and that's what matters. Our life together is what this is all about. I'm ready for anything.

And the problem we're facing now doesn't compare to the life he's promised us. I know Tatum and I know he's going to be there waiting for us.

He stands in the doorway, gripping a bouquet of my favorite flowers. A smile beams on his face, one that carries so many emotions. His eyes, filled with happy tears, welcome us home. We're home, finally home. Nothing's ever felt as sweet as this.

He wraps me in his arms and presses his lips to mine. He's proud to have me here. He's proud to be mine.

This is what home is supposed to feel like.

But sometimes dreams are just that. They try to get the better of you. And no matter how badly we want them, sometimes they're just not meant for us.

Pulling up to the gate, I see our new—*temporary*—home. It's the first time seeing it and *wow*. If this is his second home, I'd love to know what his actual house looks like.

A mansion. Sitting only feet away from the coast. Ocean water steaming the air, making it just a tiny bit easier to breathe. "Look at this place," Carson whispers to herself.

And even though the circumstances of being here aren't ideal, I can't find it in me to complain. *This place is huge!* But the feeling doesn't last for long. Tatum's car isn't here. I look for it in both driveways. I can't believe our argument has drawn us so far apart. Carson hasn't noticed and if she has, she hasn't bothered to bring it up.

"And you're mad about living here?" She laughs. It's the first time I've seen a smile on her face since before we left Leavenworth. I'm happy it's there. And it takes my mind off of Tatum, even if only for a moment.

Happiness makes Carson look different. She's almost unrecognizable. Her posture gets better. Her eyes get bigger. *She smiles*. "Where's Tatum? I thought he'd be here." She asks, finally noticing.

I wave my phone and dial his number. "Hey, where are you? We just pulled up. I'm sure you're on the way. Love you, bye."

"Voicemail?" I shake my head, yes, avoiding the rattle in my voice. We walk inside and I wait, hoping to get his call.

Tatum didn't want me living amongst Sadie's personal storage unit, yet this house seems to be the addition to that. We're practically swimming in everything she owns.

There's not a lot of chit-chat between Carson and I. She pokes around each room and chooses which one she wants to *"make her own"*. I use that term lightly as we can't make this place our own at all. We can only live amongst what's here and pull clothes from our suitcases.

Carson's back asking me where Tatum is. All I can do is

shake my head and ignore the burn crumbling me. "You want to grab some food?" I ask.

For the first time she smiles while looking at me. And I drown in the look on her face. "I thought you'd never ask," she says.

And though I wish Tatum were here with us, it's nice being alone with Carson. And it's even better that I didn't have to beg her to come out with me. Our conversations are short, but for once it feels like we have a relationship. For once it feels like she actually might like me.

TWENTY-NINE
Harper

I thought this would be different—living here so close to Tatum. We're so close to each other. I mean, shit, I'm living in his house. But there's a distance between us. One that makes forty miles feel like forever.

This place feels more like a shelter than a home. Sadie's things are everywhere. I wake up every morning and see a picture of her and Tatum on the nightstand next to where I sleep. I don't know why he hasn't taken it down yet. *I wish he would.* I can't stomach looking at it anymore and flip it upside down. Looking at the two of them smiling together hurts too much.

Getting answers out of him is near impossible. His face shows on the screen of my phone and he stares at me. He smiles as if we're all good. As if our life has started. As if we're living out everything we've ever wanted.

I don't smile back and he notes the look on my face. "How many times am I going to have to apologize?" And before I can respond he says, "This is how you're going to treat me while living in my house?"

Excuse me? "I'm not asking for another apology," I say. "Just maybe an explanation?" His voice falls silent. "Living in your house or not, I have the right to my own feelings. And if I call bullshit on a story you've concocted then I call bullshit. Deal with the consequences, Tatum."

"I've told you everything, Harper!" He yells.

"*Had to stay late at work.*" I roll my eyes. It's bullshit and he knows it. "I'd love to know the real reason. And I'd love to know why you still haven't made an effort to see me after being here for an entire week already," I say. "You realize it's been a week, right?"

"You're such a bitch," he says, turning his head away from the screen. "You're living rent free. Shit happens. Adults have things they need to worry about other than just their spouse. So stop asking so many damn questions." I'm regretting not trying to find my own place first.

His energy is so fucking draining.

Welcome home, Harper.

The distance standing between Tatum and I is cruel. It's pushing us further apart when we should be closer together. It twists my mind and shoves me into places I don't belong.

We're an hour away. *One. Hour.* Video chatting seems to be his only comfort. I moved here to be with him, not to live the life we had prior, and definitely not to live in a house that isn't mine.

I'm rocked with disappointment. Nothing is how it was supposed to be. Tatum's left both Carson and I in the dark. The confusion is rattling. He never has an answer for me.

"So when am I starting work with Tatum? I thought I was going to start right away." Carson asks. It's the first time she's mentioned part of our plan.

"He mentioned it this morning," I lie. "Should be a couple of days." She shrugs and walks away. I hate that I just lied to her, but there aren't many options to work with. And I hate that Tatum's put me in position to lose my daughters trust.

I open the sliding glass door, but Carson's so deep into the words she's writing, she doesn't even notice I'm here. She's found comfort in writing outside, listening to the water hit the rocks. I'd like to think it helps her thoughts flow easier. I mean, I've always found it easier to think standing next to the ocean. "Carson," I wave to try and get her attention. She finally looks up and gives me half a smile. But for once it doesn't seem sarcastic. "I'm going to head over to see Tatum for a little while. Will you be okay alone?" My heart beats so fast it almost feels like it's going to beat out of my chest.

"I'll be fine," she says. "Have fun."

I sit in my car staring out at the trees in front of me, wondering why it feels like I'm being pulled in one too many directions. *What the hell am I doing?*

Lying to Carson about seeing Tatum is wrong and it hurts. I can't believe it's come to this. But what happens when she notices he's not coming around? Then what am I going to tell her? How do I answer a question I don't know the answer too?

I pull out of the driveway and go. I don't know where I'm going. I wish the road led to Tatum, but I don't even know where he lives. This long, straight road seems to lead to nowhere. Maybe it leads to more places I don't belong. But still, I continue to drive.

I drove for four hours to make this lie believable. *Four hours.* Who the hell does that? But I'm back in the drive way and am dreading my conversation with Carson. I hate that I have to look her in the eyes and create a story that isn't true. But it's the only thing I can do. I don't have the strength to tell her the truth.

"That was fast," she says, looking up from her computer. "Have fun?"

I gulp. "Yeah," I say, trying to keep a steady voice. "It was nice to see him."

THIRTY
Harper

I glance down the hallway before calling Tatum, making sure Carson is in her room. Moving here has only made me feel less of a mother. There are more secrets now than ever. "What the fuck is going on?" I ask, yelling in a whisper. "You've yet to make any effort to see me."

He sighs. *Yup, sighs.*

"I've had to lie to Carson one too many times," I say. "*For you*. Telling her I'm leaving to meet you. Telling her your plans to hire her."

"I didn't ask you to lie," he says as if nothing I've said has any meaning at all. "I told you before you moved that this was a really bad time." My bones stiffen. It takes most of my strength not to blow a fuse through the top of my head.

He acts as if he didn't beg for me to come. Crying on the phone like a baby, filling me with empty promises he knew he couldn't keep. "This is your chance to be honest," I say. "Tell me why Sadie still doesn't know about us."

"I told her yesterday," he says, a little too fast. "But it's not just that, Harper. It's work. It's my kids. *It's everything*. I barely have enough time to sleep."

I shake my head. "I don't believe it," I say. My words get ahold of him. Their grip gets stronger—*tighter*. Squirming in his seat, he can't get comfortable.

"I don't know what you want me to say." His voice is low and his eyes sit in his lap. They're afraid of looking up at me. *They're afraid of the truth.* "Life throws unexpected things at us," he says. "Things we can't control." His feelings are careless and bitter. His eyes sit empty like there's no soul left to warm his cold and fragile body.

"Where do you think you're going Ms. Evans?" Ms. Peterson stands with her hand on her hip, glaring a fierce stare at Brandy and I.

Her figure is blurry. It waves from side to side. I gulp, hoping she doesn't notice the way my eyes settle from the line we just took. It's the last thing we need to be exposed and taken away.

She forces us back inside the school, escorting us to Principal Cabal's office. Biting the inside of my lip, I pray he doesn't feel the need to call my parents. My father's punishment is the last thing I need right now. They're always harsher than needed. Sometimes I wish he'd just make me kneel on dry rice for three hours. Anything is better than what he does.

"I have to call your parents," he says. My head falls into my hands. Do not cry. Do not cry. DO. NOT. CRY. I hold back the urge as best as I can.

These are the moments I thank this powdery substance for. It makes the pain bearable. It makes me feel like I'll make it out of this. It's my favorite killer.

Wren sits outside the office with a smug look on her face. Tatum's next to her. "Might want to smarten up, Evans," she says. "If you actually want to make something of yourself, coming to school might be a start." Brandy pulls my backpack, stopping me from lunging at her—to stop my hands from mangling her pretty face into something no one wants to see. It's hard to believe the person she's turned out to be.

The bell rings, but I stay late to get help for one of the classes

I'm failing. If there's anything I need more than to wrap each of my fingers around Wren's throat, it's graduating to get the hell out of this school and to move away to college. I need to get away from this place. These people. This town. My parents.

Wrens alone in the parking lot. I'm not sure what for, but she sees me and rolls her eyes. My body fills with rage and it's out of control. It consumes me and there's no stopping it.

I sneak up behind her. My fists are hard. My knuckles are white. Every punch is more liberating than the last. The lump growing inside of me clogs my throat. My best friend has turned into my worst enemy. How could she do this to me? I want to stop, but I can't. And she can't get a grip on me. She can't even throw a single punch.

From the corner of my eye, I notice a small body. Tatum. *Our eyes meet. I stop for a moment wondering what it is he'll try to do to me for beating up his girlfriend.* His eyes sit empty like there's no soul left to warm his cold and fragile body. *He slips away without doing anything.* Nothing at all. Wren doesn't see him. She doesn't see that he's left her here to rot.

To bleed.
To hurt.
All alone.

Tatum's face shows up on my phone screen. I'm not in the mood to listen to the harsh words he wants to say. I press the F U button on him. He can unclog the grime filling his bones another time.

Tatum: You guys need to leave.
Me: What?
Tatum: Sadie's going to the house for a girl's weekend. I'm sorry, Harper. I didn't tell her you were there.

THIRTY-ONE
Harper

There was a small hotel fifteen minutes down the street Carson and I were able to go to. I don't dare look at her. I can't bear the judgment growing in her eyes. "At least we have an ocean view," she says. I shrug and say nothing back. We had an ocean view where we were.

"I'm sorry." She says it like she feels bad for me, which only makes me feel worse.

"Not your fault." I throw myself on the bed and close my eyes, trying to rub away my headache and hoping the pit in my stomach doesn't surface. "I should be the one who's sorry."

"You haven't done anything wrong." There's a shriek in her voice. Even she knows that's not true. I've done a lot of things wrong—too many for me to count, too many for her to count.

"I shouldn't have dragged you here," I tell her. "If I knew we'd be living in a house amongst so many things—*too many things*, we wouldn't have come. I know you gave up a lot to live here."

"There's a lot of shit in that house," she laughs and I start to laugh with her. It feels good to finally be able to laugh about something with Carson. And since it's something we rarely do together, I hold on to it just a little bit longer. "You know you don't have to apologize," she says after the moment is washed away. "This move was very..." she pauses and shrugs. "Very different than what we planned. I—I'm sorry he's put us through this."

For a moment, I can see why life has brought me here. Because even if just for a moment, these four, dingy, hotel walls have helped knock down Carson's wall. And while the air is stale, our relationship's expiration date seems to be getting further away.

"You don't need that stupid job," I say, thinking of all the promises Tatum has muffled. She nods her head, but she has nothing left to say. And I'm okay with it because for once I saw a side of my daughter I haven't seen in so long.

Reality doesn't take long to set back in. There's a stillness in silence that brings out the harsh side of reality. And it's here and thriving. I'm lying on a bed in a hotel room. I'm not sure it's the cleanest, but it's a roof over our heads.

What the fuck is happening? Too many thoughts circle. It's a constant merry-go-round with Tatum. His words don't sit well and it's hard not to assume there's something he's not telling me. I look Sadie up on Facebook and I'm already regretting it staring at her profile picture. It's been updated since the last time I checked.

It's her.

And Tatum.

And their two kids.

The four of them pose in the front entrance of Disney, smiling. Tatum's arm wraps around her waist as if he's proud she's his wife. *Like he's lucky.*

Staring into the screen of a face that's supposed to make me smile, I find my sight starting to blur. Tears cram into my eyes as I read the caption that goes along with this picture-perfect family. *Perfect day with the most perfect people.*

My tears plunge onto the screen and their faces start to fade. My stomach rots in a pit of disgust. Why bring me here? Why bring my daughter here?

I search for their divorce. It's public record, so I should be able to find it. I click and click and click. Page after page. Line after line. There is nothing, absolutely nothing on the Sadie and Tatum Barne's divorce. *Nothing.* It feels as if all our love has been grappled and shredded and thrown into the mere existence of space so we can never reach it again.

I focus my stare on Carson. She's lying on her back, face glowing from the light on her computer screen. Her face is scrunched with lines shaping her face.

I wonder what her book is like. What does she hide in between her words? There must be parts of her undying truth woven between each and every word. She writes more than she talks. It's where she feels most at home—*the safest.* I'm glad she has a safe space to live in. It's something I needed when I was her age.

"Wanna take a break?" I ask.

"Can't." Her eyes refuse to look away.

"Even if Tatum does offer you the job," I say. "If he ever does. I don't think you should take it."

Her eyes find the courage to break free from the screen and stare back at me. "Why would I do that?" And though I want to tell her I don't think the job was ever going to be a reality, I also don't want her to stop writing. I've never seen her move quite like this.

"Focus on your book," I say.

"And stop paying my bills?" She asks. "Yeah, no thank you."

And knowing it'll be a struggle, I promise her I'll take care of her. "Your book is what's most important." Carson just shakes her head. She doesn't give me an answer and I don't ask for one. She's back to writing. And I'm back to being swallowed up by our new reality.

Calling Tatum out is the only way we can move on. It's the only way I can get any sort of answer. *Hopefully.* My fingers move across the screen, forming words I never wanted to say. I can't call. I won't.

I'm afraid of my own voice.
Maybe that's why Carson writes so much. Maybe after all these years of assuming we have nothing in common, we actually do. It's just we're so afraid of using our voice. Is that a legal phobia? *It should be.*

You live a life of lies. How can anyone be so evil? You dragged me down here with no intention of being with me. It's obvious. You live a double life and thought you'd get away with it. Does the thought of having two women get you off? Does it make you feel superior? Do you need to feel in control because your entire life growing up slipped through your fingers? I changed my life for you. I uprooted everything for you. How could you do this to me? To my family? To us? I thought I was something to you, but I'm nothing, obviously. You have a perfect family. You have two kids and a wife. Maybe we should end this. Maybe I should just go home.

The tiny word *delivered* pops up on the bottom of the screen. My stomach sinks and my mouth fills with an irony taste I almost can't stomach. My phone starts to ring, but I end the call before it can start.

Please call me. His text begs.

The three words sprawled across the screen make me cringe. Having to listen to his excuses, having to *use my voice*—I don't know. I don't know what to do.

More texts come through. He's begging for a call. He's begging for me to answer. Each message tortures me a little more than the last.

I'm caving.

"You have to believe me," he says when I finally answer. "She's crazy. She's trying to convince her family we're still together. I promise, Harper, it's not what it looks like." His voice, so accusing, pushes me far away from what I know is true.

What would be his reason to bring me here if they're still married? Forcing me away from my state, my home, for what? To make fun of me for believing in love again? A sensible person wouldn't do that. *He wouldn't do that, right?*

"I don't understand," I say. "So you spent the day with her at Disney to convince her family you're together?" My nails dig into the palm of my hand, resisting the burn scorching my throat. "Just tell me the truth."

"It was a family day," he finally admits. His eyes look nowhere in my direction. "I promise it's not what you think."

"Bullshit," I say. My tone feeds the burn.

His eyes feed off the fire pouring out of my pores. "Unlike you, I want my kids to experience life with both parents around. It's called co-parenting." My back straightens. "Sorry your kid's father doesn't give a shit about them. I care about my kids," he says. "And as much as I hate Sadie, we always put our feelings aside when it comes to them. Something you and your ex-husband have failed to do for your own."

"Don't you dare bring my family into this." My teeth grit together. "You lied to me, Tatum. Family day or not. Feelings set aside or not. That's not what you told me you were doing."

He shakes his head as if I'm the liar. "You're just as crazy as her," he says.

"Then call me crazy," I say. "And maybe I'll give her a call and ask her what's going on. I mean you seem to have a hard time giving me the truth. How the fuck do I know what else you've lied about?"

His eyes, cold and devoid, invade my personal space. "And you think you'll get something out of her?" He laughs. It's so sinister, it stings. "She has every reason to lie to you," he says. "She'll do anything to get back together with me. She'll destroy your mind, Harper. Don't forget that."

As if I'm not already damaged.

Picking up the phone, I call Brandy just to hear a familiar voice. I'm not planning on letting her in on the tragedies of my new life. And though she's the least judgmental person I know, judgment has to surface sometimes.

It must.

"Are you okay?" She asks. Having been able to perfect the act of masking my feelings, I'm shocked she's able to see through me. "Tell me what's wrong," she says. It's debilitating having to sort through the things I should and shouldn't say. "You can trust me, Harper."

She's the only one I can trust. But admitting failure isn't painless. How do you come clean so easily? People use their eyes to shove you further down the rabbit hole as if you can't see the judgment living inside of them.

Looking around, *it hits me.* I'm lying on a hotel bed to hide. I'm hiding from a woman I don't even know. Tatum's hiding me away. My tongue starts to tell Brandy the beginning of the story, but each word reveals more of the truth.

"Come home," she whispers. "Everyone misses you." But this isn't a vacation. This is my life now. Getting up to leave isn't an option. *It can't be.*

I almost ask how my mom is, but the truth might make me want to leave after all. I've been living for my parents all these years and today feels no different.

"I can't," I say in a voice that fades away. "I have nothing but constant reminders of what my life was before."

"But your dad can't hurt you anymore, Harper," she says. "His hands can't reach you. *He's gone.*"

Excuse me? Part of my brain stutters trying to process the words she just let out of her mouth. I fall back into a cold shadow and close my eyes.

This is impossible.
She can't know.

"What are you talking about?" I ask.

She gulps, loudly. "I-I didn't mean it like that," she stammers. But she did mean it like that. *She knows.* How the hell does she know?

"Tell me now," my voice shakes, strung with humiliation. Hiding in the corner is my morale, scared of ever showing my face again. If she knows...who else knows?

"Your brother," she says. The words whisper out of her

mouth, but it doesn't soften the pain of the stab.

Rage infiltrates the depths of my bones. Carson sits still while her mouth hangs open. "They've been sleeping together," I say. The back of my throat is torn apart from the scorch of my voice.

Pacing back and forth, I attempt to wrap my head around the damage she's provoked. Her calls keep coming through, attempting to make excuses.

End.

End.

End!

"Since high school," I whisper. "They've been doing this since fucking high school." Carson hasn't said much. I don't think she knows what to say. *I don't know what to say.*

Adam's abuse is no stranger to Brandy. She's witnessed his antics—felt the wrath of his words—and still, she decided to confide in him. *So much for trust.*

I wish I had my mom right now. I wish she had her mind. I wish she were a mother who cared a little bit more. I wish she loved me a little bit more. I call her anyway, just to hear her voice. Just to pretend for a moment she's all I need.

"I miss you," I say.

"When will you be home?" My heart falls to my stomach. She's forgotten that I've moved. Failure rings even louder in my ear, reminding me I'm still stuffed with mistake.

I've abandoned my family.

"This is my home now." I'm wrapped in a blend of emotions I don't feel like sorting through. I hold back everything I want to say. Things I probably should, but won't.

Whispers come from the other side of the phone, but I can't make out what she's saying. "You okay, Ma?"

"It's nothing, Harper," she says. "I'm just talking to your father. He wants to know how you're doing." *My father?*

How far away is she?

Here lies a man who is lanky, bald, and dressed like a preacher. I've spent thirty-six years looking at him, but yet, I can't recognize the face looking back at me.

A slow suffering pains me. We're face to face with death and life all at once. Our morals and life experiences were always polar opposites. He wanted different for me. He wanted a better life, but he failed to acknowledge what made me happy was what I already had.

I wish we had a different outcome. A different life. A better relationship. Being able to coddle the love of my father is something I've always dreamed of. But now, staring at his lifeless body, it's something I'll never be able to touch.

My eyes swell not for the pain of his passing, but the pain of what we never had. "I'm sorry, Dad," I say. "I'm sorry we could never be the person we needed for each other."

I wonder what he'd think of me now. *Living with a man.* Well—*almost*. Would he stand proud or sulk with disgust in my decision to leave part of my family behind?

My mind gets caught in the web of the past, teetering back and forth with *what if's*. Living in my parents' discomfort can't be something I settle for. The person they wanted me to be is different than who I *need* to be.

Maybe this has been my problem all along. Maybe this is what holds me back—*the grip of who I 'should've been'*. Maybe Tatum is as innocent as he's making himself seem. Maybe I'm the one searching for a problem that isn't there.

Maybe...I'm the problem.

THIRTY-TWO
Harper

There's a hunger for settlement lingering. The knot in my throat feels more like vomit than the need to cry. Tatum should be here any minute. Overthinking is my own worst enemy. Do I hug him? Kiss him? Sit and do nothing? *He's here.*

There's hope inside of me that thinks seeing Tatum will heal all of our problems. There's hope that when he sees me—when he holds me—he'll remember exactly what he loves so much about me.

He leans in for a hug that lasts only for a short moment. Kissing my lips doesn't cross his mind. Instead, he sits across from me and waits for me to do the talking. But he has no idea how afraid I am to use my voice.

I press my lips into a straight line and close my eyes. I'm going to have to use my voice because as of now, he's not talking. "I don't want to argue," I say.

"Lately, it seems like that's all you want to do," he replies. "I still love you, Harper. But learning how to balance my kids, work and you has been hard for me. I don't want to be the kind of father my dad was."

There it is. The answer I've been looking for. "Why haven't

you said anything, Tatum? We're supposed to be a team and work together towards things that make us feel good. Keeping your problems to yourself is only straining our relationship."

He nods and closes his eyes. "I'm embarrassed," he whispers. His head sulks in the palm of his hand as if he has a million more things on his mind, but he needs to let them out. It's the only way we can make this work. "I'm sorry," he says. "This isn't how I planned things." His voice fades as if what's on his chest is going to kill both of us.

Spit it out.

"I haven't been completely honest," he says, adjusting himself in his seat. "Sadie and I aren't divorced yet." The court records proved this to me, but hearing it from his mouth makes it that much more real.

All the things he's ever said—*promised*—vanish into nothing. Everything feels like a lie. Sitting without movement, I try to collect my thoughts into something more manageable. His eyes poke and beg for me to say something, anything at all.

The picture of them, the one that started all of this, flares back into my mind. I'm able to conjure up the smaller details. She wore her wedding ring, proudly, with her arm hugging his waist.

It all makes sense now.

They're married.

Actually married.

It's hard to believe I've been naïve enough to trust his words, naïve enough to move away from my family, my friends, *my daughter*. He should've gone with an acting career instead. It suits him better than trying to fix people's mobility.

"But we're separated," he says, trying to convince me their marriage is nothing but a piece of paper. But it's going to take more than that to convince me.

I work up the courage to ask a question I'm scared to know the answer to. "Do you want her back?" He swallows the lump in his throat, almost hesitating. Nodding my head, I understand his answer without hearing the words he should say.

Words I deserve to hear.

Words I need to hear.

"Why did you do all of this?" I ask.

"Do what?"

"Beg me." My voice sharpens. "Beg me and my daughter to move down here and create a fantasy out of us. To promise her a job and never follow through? How could you do that?"

He bites his bottom lip. "Sadie still works there." My jaw clenches. Fooling me is one thing, but fooling my daughter is another. "But I love you, Harper."

A caustic laugh bursts from my throat. "You love me?"

"Of course I do," he says, tucking his chin into his neck. "I don't want her back. I want you back."

"Then prove it," I say.

"I'm afraid," he whispers. "She threatens to take my kids away. I can't be my father, Harper. I just can't." Facing your past isn't comfortable. Avoiding it may be easier, but it destroys everything in its path.

Everything.

THIRTY-THREE

Sadie

August sits across from me in my hotel room. Both of us have our clothes on. Neither of us wants to speak. And we both refuse to make eye contact. My stare is steady on his hand, watching as he lifts his cup of gin to his lips. I wonder how the bitter taste makes his mind spin.

Ten years ago we found ourselves in a similar situation. Except, that time we were here to celebrate Wiley's birthday, not praying for her life. And we may have had less control over our actions then, too.

There's an ache that burns the back of my throat. *Tell him the truth*. If there were a time for honesty, now would be a perfect time. We don't know how much time we have. We don't know if we'll live to see tomorrow.

He deserves the truth.

He looks over at me as if he heard the words in my head. "I know you're not happy with him," he says as if that's a normal thing an ex-husband should say. "Don't hate Wiley," he says, stopping for a moment as if he needs an extra moment to breathe—an extra moment to think about what he should say—about what he *shouldn't* say. "She's told me almost everything."

My stomach drops. *Except for the reason I cheated on you.* He must find humor in the fact that my marriage walks all over me. I look up to meet his gaze, but he's already looked away. "There is truth in the words he says, whether they're to you or someone else." He knows about Tatum's thumbs dancing. Why else would he say that? "But you can always find the truth, Sadie. You just have to look for it." Hearing his voice, raspy and drowning in gin, almost makes me fall apart.

Almost makes me fall in love.

Almost.

But watching as his brows move to the rhythm of his thoughts, I realize it may already be too late.

I've searched for the truth. I've scrounged for the truth. I've even hid the truth. I'd tell him, but the words rather sit in silence.

I rather sit in silence.

In pain.

In woe.

THIRTY-FOUR
Sadie

Wiley's stable, but my mind can't get over the thought of what tomorrow may bring. And sitting back home, where Tatum's back sleeping, doesn't feel right.

Budging himself back into this house, making it his home—*again*—isn't what I want. Refusing to give me space is only suffocating me. It's only making me want to run. Subjecting myself to fall back into Tatum's merry-go-round will destroy me.

I can't fall back.

I won't. Not this time.

August told me to find the truth. And I did. Well sort of. I'm working on it. There is truth in the texts he sends. I just need to see them *before* they're deleted. Did you know our phones carry everything we want to keep hidden? None of it is ever deleted. *Ever.*

Part of me doesn't want to barge in and demand to see the messages my husband has been sending to entertain stray women. But this isn't a matter of wanting anymore. I deserve the truth and it doesn't matter if Tatum believes that or not.

This is our final moment.

Staring at the pages, I'm ready for this new path I need to

Dear Tatum

take. Hundreds of pages are waiting for me. Line by line I learn something new. Line by line I learn Alisa wasn't the only one who fell victim to Tatum's scheme, but she was one of the more serious flings he had going on.

Alisa: i can't believe she almost caught us.

Tatum: she told me you were having sex with your boyfriend. almost slipped and said it was me.

Alisa: you should've.

Tatum: i'm not ready yet. she'll flip and try to take the kids away from me.

Alisa: i'll always be here for you. I love u Tatum.

Tatum: Thanks.

He's someone else on this phone—a man I can hardly recognize. Manipulating the same women he charms—taking full advantage of their disadvantages. He's putting on a show to dance a dance he doesn't know.

Harper.
Harper.
Harper.
Harper.

Here's another woman whose name pops up more than Alisa. It's a constant back and forth between them. Mere minutes pass until they're back looking at their phone's responding to one another.

Harper: i love you so much.

Tatum: me too.

Every day, every hour is another I love you, another I miss you. I've never caught a glimpse of this woman before. *Never.* She's faceless, living a lie with *my* husband.

Harper: i can't wait until we're living together. i'm happy Carson's finally on board to move down there.

Tatum: it's going to be perfect.

Two worlds. Tatum's been living in two different worlds. Keeping up must be harder than he thought it'd be. There's years worth of messages between them.
    He's kinder to Harper. He engages in what he wants for *their* future together. He goes to visit her when he needs to go to… Washington.
    To work.
    Leavenworth.
    She's from his hometown.
    They must have… *grown up together.*
    It all makes sense. No wonder Charlotte's graduation was a second thought to him. Boning his long-distance girlfriend is the top of his priority list. Let that one sink in.
    Fights. Arguments. It's all part of a real relationship and that's exactly what this is. They've argued over me. *Me.* He's slandered my name, spewed harsh fiction about who '*I am*'. Lying about *everything*.
    This woman's secrets are here to be read. To be heard. To be felt. The worst thing she could've done is confided in him, yet that's all she does. He reciprocates with lies, reeling her in even further. She falls for the dance. She grabs his hand and swings on

his swing, never thinking she'd be the one to fall.

Sorting the pages of Alisa and Harper, I realize Alisa never stopped seeing Tatum. Their last message was... *last night.* He was smooth enough to reel her back in? For God's sake, what kind of power does this man hold over her? I rummage through. I need to find something, anything to help untangle their riddle.

> Tatum: i'm leaving disney now.
> Alisa: what? how come? thought you wanted to spend time with the kids.
> Tatum: i miss you, and sadie and harper are driving me crazy.
> Alisa: when does she arrive?
> Tatum: 5pm she's staying at the beach house. don't know where else to put her.
> Alisa: send her ass back home.
> Tatum: wish i could. coming to see you. leaving now.

The beach house.
Our beach house?
Our home.

She's made a nest of my home. They've made love in the same bed as us. I've spent the last five summers there making memories with Tatum and our kids. *Everything is stained.* The memories are fading too fast for me to catch. Sick to my stomach, I hold my hand over my mouth and close my eyes.

Tatum is a monster.

His web of lies unravels, and leave me accompanied only by my own shadow. Lies fall off his tongue like it's natural. And the truth leaves me breathless. I'm finding the answer to the equation—*finally.*

Staying with Tatum would only mean I'm letting my kids down. He's the last kind of person I'd want my kids to end up with. What would I be telling them? That love is a constant game of close your eyes and pretend you didn't see? I'd be transferring this frail version of love to another generation, only for them to suffer, too.

Taking my faults and allowing them to dress me is the only way I'll be able to make it out of this. They're everything that's held me back. But my faults are just that, *faults*. And trying to take them back will only rip away my right to breathe. I'm not perfect and I'll never claim to be, but there's finally an edge to what I can take and I'm standing on it.

Hiding my emotions is one of my specialties. And controlling who I am is one of theirs. They're the root of all my problems and the solution to all my problems. I just need to speak.

I need to use my voice.

I need to find it.

Being silent has killed a part of me. My pain has muted my truth and forced me to a place I don't want to be. But today is the day I take my voice back.

Today, my voice belongs to me.

THIRTY-FIVE
Sadie

Aiming my shot at Harper is the last thing I need to do. I need to aim at the right person to get the best shot—*Tatum.*

The door slams shut. I look up from my phone to see Tatum throwing his bags down on the floor. "Isn't your apartment meant for you to live there?" He looks up at me and tilts his head. "Why do you continue to come around?"

"Are you okay?" He asks.

"Perfectly fine," I say. "Just want to know why you stopped living at your apartment."

"Because I thought…" He looks around, confusion riddles through him. "I thought we were trying to work things out." His voice narrows as if he's asking a question.

"We were, Tatum," I say, keeping my voice stern. "Then I learned the truth," I laugh. "Well, part of it."

He shrugs as if he has no idea what I'm talking about. He shrugs as if my words come as a surprise.

"Why are you still fucking Alisa?"

He nearly chokes on his own spit. "Excuse me?" I raise an eyebrow in response. "Why would you think that?" He tries to torture me with crooked truth. But text messages don't lie. And I won't continue to close my eyes to the truth.

"And who the fuck is Harper and why is she living in my house?" His skin falls bleak realizing the nightmare of all his secrets sprouting to the surface is coming true.

"I don't know what you're talking about." He's trying to brush off his twisted reality as if it's only a fantasy he wishes to live in. But I wave the proof I have in his face, letting it rot in his eyes. "You're fucking crazy," he says. "You have no idea what privacy is."

"Maybe not," I laugh. "But maybe I'm just desperate for some truth since it seems like you're unable to tongue any sincerity."

He shields himself with an emotionless mask. His eyes carry an empty load of feeling. They're cold and dark. I've watched this side of him come alive many times before. It's here to protect him—to shield outsiders from the truth. The truth being, *he's scared*. Scared of all the pain that's cradled by honesty. But what scares him most is he knows he won't be able to talk me out of it, even if he tries.

"I'll be staying at my apartment tonight," he says, straightening his back as if that'll tear me down. "And until you're done believing the bullshit lies of...*that*." He points to the stack of *proof*. "Then maybe we can have a discussion on how we can move on in this marriage."

He walks away and out of the front door like he won something. As if having the last word would make me question reality. Giving him that power, I keep my mouth closed and let him soak in it. He'll feel my burn sooner rather than later. It's already creeping up on him waiting to shake him out of his wits. Laughing at that will be the ultimate satisfaction. And the look on his face will be even better.

Pulling up to a home that once belonged to me slashes the inside of my stomach. And legally it's still mine, but it feels so far away from my heart. The rush of excitement I normally feel pulling

Dear Tatum

into the driveway is blocked with a wound that invades most of my being.

Tears gather at the brim of my eyes holding most of my discomfort. My house key burns a hole in my pocket, reminding me that everything has changed. Nothing is what it once was and it will never be the same.

I stand limp, staring at the front door. I'm inches away from barging in and demanding Harper to give back what is mine. But I hadn't thought ahead to this moment. Using my key doesn't feel right. And knocking on my own front door isn't normal. But Harper's made this her nest—*her home.*

And though it's hard not to point the finger at her, it's not her fault. She's not the root of Tatum and I's evil. He is. Tatum's the claw of the devil's hand and I won't put that kind of blame on a woman who was lied to by a man she loves. She's just another victim in his trap.

Silence begins to sting the inside of my ears before I decide to knock. It's a hard, yet friendly knock, but no one answers. Looking around I see a black car sitting in the driveway.

"She has to be here," I whisper to myself.

The frosted glass get's darker before I realize someone's coming. A deep breath is crucial to my well-being. I close my eyes and reopen them when I hear the door creak open.

"Hi, Sadie," Harper says. I stand, motionless, unable to move hearing my name spill off her tongue. But knowing my name isn't the most surprising thing about her.

It's the way she looks. Stress wears her. Pre-existing wrinkles line her face, but don't consume her beauty. She's short, about 5'3", with blonde hair that sits on her shoulders. She's neither a model nor a grisly.

Her flaws are highlighted by her polish. They seem to be what make her. And she radiates a kind of beauty one may find untraditional.

She reminds me of...*me.*

I'm not sure what attracts Tatum to Harper. His mistresses are women you find in magazines. Women that try to set unreasonable standards for beauty. Long, toned legs. Long dark hair. Flawless, wrinkle-free skin. And a stomach that barfs at the thought of a stretchmark.

"You must be Harper." The words come out awkward and botched and she doesn't say anything back. She just stares, mouth slightly ajar, as if she's in shock I'm standing in front of her.

She opens the door wider and stands to the side to let me in. Being inside is even worse than being outside. Who serves who? Where do I sit? Everything is so unsettling.

"Want a drink?" She cowers making note of our current posture. She's tamer than I thought she'd be and I'm not sure why. But then again, I'm not sure about a lot of things right now. All I know is the shake in my hands isn't showing any signs of stopping.

Harper approaches the table with two cups of water and takes a seat across from me. I'm ready to find out the truth. The words, *I'm sorry*, start to slip from her mouth, but I stop her before they're all the way out.

"It's okay," I say, even though we both know nothing about this is okay. We linger in the silence pressing us together. And I don't know about her, but the silence is burning me alive. All the rage I thought I'd feel, seeing her in the flesh, falls apart.

"I need to apologize," she says, slicing through the lull we're drowning in. And even though, I didn't come here for an apology, it's nice to hear.

We start to fall into the game he's thrown us both in. Trying to figure out what each piece means and why. Once the awkward stage fades, our voices start to be put to good use. The more Harper says, the more I realize how similar Tatum has groomed us. Twisting what hurts us most into something only he can bandage and make better.

"Who is Carson?" I ask.

Her head falls to her lap. "My daughter," she says, disappointed. "Tatum promised her a job here," she says. "She quit her job and lost her promotion." Staring at Harper with my mouth hitting the floor, I try to comprehend the act in which Tatum took to make this world believable. Putting not only Harper in a horrible position but her daughter? What kind of man does that?

He's turning out to be more of a monster than I ever thought. He hurts without feeling. He stabs and pokes the people who love him most, right when they turn their back. It's mortifying to think anyone could be so cruel.

"Do you know about Alisa?"

"His assistant?" She asks. "Yeah. He's told me the two of you have—" Her voice starts to fade. "Have fallen apart because you think they're..."

"They are," I say, seeing where she's going with this. "I confronted her a while back. She promised to stay away, but their texts prove something different."

She groans, while rubbing her eyes. Learning about one betrayal is hard to digest, imagine two. It's less shocking to me, of course. Him and I have been here before—one too many times. But Tatum and Harper? I don't think she's seen this side of him.

"Alisa knows about both of us," I say. "Something's weird about the two of them together. I mean, fuck, she's half his age and doesn't care he's cheating on his wife."

"What do you think is going on?"

I shake my head. "The only way to find out is to ask."

"Not Tatum," she says.

"You'd have to be messed up to think you could ask him." We both laugh, *together*. And though it's only for a short moment, it's nice to be able to find common ground with Harper.

"I'm sorry he's put you through this," I say, knowing that even though she's laughing now, the truth always finds a way to torment the most vulnerable.

She shrugs. "I was gay before I met Tatum." *Wait, what?* "Still am?" There's uncertainty in her voice. "I am gay. I like women. But falling in love with Tatum," she pauses. "It just—it just felt right, but yet so wrong." She looks down at her lap, avoiding the possibility of what's true being seen through her eyes. "I'm so used to doing the wrong thing, ya know? I thought maybe...he'd be the one." There is clear pain living in her eyes. It's dancing to confuse her, to hurt her. Watching it play even hurts a part of me. Life can be so cruel sometimes.

"There were a lot of things that didn't add up to me. But pushing Tatum in the wrong direction would've destroyed the fantasy I had for us. *For me.*" She shrugs. "Maybe my dreams were bigger than his. Maybe I thought one day he'd wake up and realize I was the one he wanted and everything that was against us would somehow manage to disappear."

The sound of her voice, the way her words piece together, it buries an ache under my skin. And it's not just because Tatum's my husband, but because of how rich her pain is. Tatum destroyed her. There are frail and fragile cracks lining her, just waiting to fall apart. He's brought her to an edge she shouldn't be on, just how he did to me. "Do you want to come with me to see Alisa?"

"Really?" She asks.

"You deserve answers too," I say. "We both do."

THIRTY-SIX
Sadie

Alisa stands behind the front desk staring at Harper and I, mouth ajar and skin so pale it looks like she's going to faint.

"Let's go," I say. "Now."

There's a willingness to her, almost like she thinks making the wrong move will send her into a pit. She moves swiftly, grabbing her purse, placing the papers in her hand down, only to then push in her chair to come stand in front of us. "Where are we going?" She asks, not looking as timid. It's almost as if she's been waiting all day for this very moment.

The stupid smirk on her face sends my world into a tunnel of hate. The palm of my hand presses to her shoulder and I push with all the strength I have left. "What the fuck was that for?" She asks, acting like we're dumb as if she has no idea what's going on. It only angers me more and we haven't even made it out of Tatum's office yet.

"You know what that was for," Harper says.

"What's going on between you and him?" I ask, nodding towards his office.

"Who's *him*?" She's still trying to play us like we're stupid.

Gripping the collar of her shirt, Harper pulls her back up. "Tatum, bitch. That's who." I'm impressed by Harper's will to give Alisa a little of what she deserves. She seemed so fragile before this.

"I rather not do this here," she says.

We end up at the Coffee Bean, where Harper and I will finally get our truth. "Lay it out," I say the moment we reach our table. There is no more time for silence. No more time to keep swimming in this twisted, fucked up game Tatum's started.

Harper sits next to me and her stare is pinching Alisa. Alisa's shoulders tense and she's breathing heavier. I think the truth of it all is finally getting to her. "Remember when you came to see me?"

I nod.

"Well a couple of days later, I went to drop something off on his desk and there was a word document open," she pauses. "It caught the corner of my eye and what I saw made me a little sick." My imagination flowers, and my stomach knots. "Sadie," she says, looking at me, and then turning to Harper. "He never got a slot in the convention. It was all made up."

"Alisa, I saw the letter," I say. She reaches into her purse, pulling out the same folder she had in the office. In it is Tatum's acceptance letter. It's highlighted and noted with a handful of grammar errors. "No professional is going to make these kinds of mistakes." Everything around me falls into a void I can no longer see. *Everything is red.* Tatum's acceptance letter was a fake. A fucking fake.

Just.

Like.

Him.

"Wait," Harper says. "If he didn't get into the convention then...?"

"Where was he?" I finish Harper's thought. Wherever it is, it better be good. He chose that over his daughter. "Thanks," I say, getting ready to leave.

"That's not everything. You should sit back down." Her

words yank me back into my seat, even though I want to run away and never look back. "I confronted Tatum about this."

"You did?" I ask, more surprised she found it in her to stand up to him. Before all of this, she was delicate and brittle, always afraid of doing something to get herself fired.

"He begged me not to tell," she pauses. "But my silence came with a price." I gulp down the knot in my throat. "I told him he needed to pay my rent." A piece of her voice holds a handful of shame. "He was my only chance at surviving." *Sneaky, yet clever.* "And as time went on we ended up getting back together," she winces. "But it was more of an open relationship. And with my apartment down the street from your house, it was easy for him to leave whenever the two of you would argue." My stomach plummets and it feels like I'm going to vomit.

"Down the street?" I ask, mostly mumbling to myself. "Was he living with you?" She shakes her head, yes.

Damn it, Tatum.

THIRTY-SEVEN
Sadie

A single piece of paper lies in between the tips of my fingers. This used to hold the meaning of my marriage. It used to promise me everything would work out. Now, all it does is remind me of the torture I put myself through. Our marriage certificate has done nothing but silence me. It's stripped me of my voice. It combined two voices into one. *Marriage should never be one voice.*

Up and down, side to side, I rip apart the only thing keeping me tied to Tatum. Thinking about how happy this makes me cracks me up. Laughter pours out like it's never flowed before. Ripping this up means nothing to the law. I'll still need to file for divorce, but right now, I am full.

Full of thoughts.
Full of bliss.
Full of things I need and want to do.

But it all comes crashing down when I hear a noise coming from behind me. I turn my head to find Tatum standing in the doorway. His eyes are bloodshot and brimming with tears. "What is that?" He asks, but I don't have to tell him. He knows what it is. "Harper called me." *Fucking, Harper.* I roll my eyes. He steps towards me and crumbles to his knees, pleading for forgiveness. His charade makes me cringe. "What are we going to do?" He cries.

"I don't know what you're going to do," I say. "But I know what I'm going to do." It takes most of my will power not to give in and cry with him. This is the end of an era. The end of a piece of me. No matter how bad things are, leaving is always a hard goodbye.

Staring at me with tears blurring his vision, he waits for me to tell him my plans. He waits for me to fall back into the game. The fantasy. *But I don't.*

I fall into his eyes. I fall into the place where he hides his pain, debating whether or not to admit my faults now. I want to. I need to. But I'm afraid. I'm afraid of what he'll do to me. I'm afraid of what he'll do to my kids.

"I'm divorcing you," I say. Screams belch from deep in his chest, piercing my ears. He falls to the floor and throws a tantrum like he's some five-year-old boy not getting the toy he wants.

"No, Sadie. We will fix this. I'll change. Please don't do this to our family."

There are a lot of things I could say but don't. "I don't love you anymore, Tatum." Loving a woman doesn't involve sleeping with others. Tatum may love me, but it's not for the right reasons. He loves my convenience. To have a wife is to show off a stable life. It's to have a beautiful woman stand next to you in the public eye. To make you feel like you have it all together, even though you know deep down, you don't.

Watching him unravel piece by piece hurts so much. And it's not because I'll miss him, but because he's human too, and pain is pain. It always hurts.

I pound my fist against the door, hoping the right person opens it. Silence rings, so I knock again.

"Sadie?" August stands in front of me, hair out of place with nothing but a pair of boxers on. I bite my lip and stop my mind from wandering to the times I used to dance on that body. "How did you—"

"I paid twenty bucks to a random website to find your address." He laughs and swings the door open wider, inviting me in.

"I'm all ears," he says.

His gaze is heavy and his eyes are stuck to me, just waiting for what it is I have to confess. Choking on my words, I try to spit out the right ones, knowing this is my only chance. "I love you, August. And I'm sorry for what I did fifteen years ago. I've regretted it every day since." I bite my lip and run my fingers through my hair. "I'm not excusing my behavior, but there were reasons behind what I did. Reasons I wish I handled differently."

He cuts me off before I finish. "Did you and Tatum get into a fight?" I should tell the truth. He deserves it, but it wasn't really a fight. It was the search for the truth and I found it. But I'm not sure it'll sound convincing.

"I left him," I say. "And this brings me to the point I was trying to say earlier. You're everything I want. You're what I've needed all along. And I can't hide it anymore." He doesn't smile. He doesn't lean in for a hug to squeeze me and whisper how much he's missed me. He does none of that. In fact, he doesn't look excited at all. His eyebrows are drawn straight. His lips curl downwards and his eyes fall dark. The room spins around us as he thinks about what it is he needs to say.

Flicking me out of this trance is a loud thud coming from his bedroom. My head jerks towards the door to see what it is, but when I hear a voice yell, *sorry babe*, I knew it was time to go.

"I'm sorry, Sadie," he says, walking behind me.

"Me too."

And that was it. That's all he had to say. There was no pulling of the hand as I walked away. No passionate kiss at the end of the driveway.

This is real life, not a fairytale. But, August deserves his fairytale. It just sucks I can't be the one to give it to him, but I'm faulty.

Dear Tatum

I have my kids and me to take care of, and that's enough for right now. I can handle that. The next chapter of my life will probably be the most challenging yet, and it'll be full of change. But isn't that what we need in order to grow?

Change makes us better people. And as much as we're scared of it, it's the one thing that never fails us. Change helps us breathe again.

I can finally breathe, again.

THIRTY-EIGHT
Harper

Being home is bittersweet, but Carson and I needed this visit. It's a touch of what used to be to help ease the bullshit we've been living in. There's a piece of me rooted here in Leavenworth that won't ever leave, no matter how hard I try to pull away.

Carson and I walk into the house to find everyone we love waiting for us. There are decorations and food and desserts. *There are people smiling.* Being embraced by family and friends is exactly what I needed. It was also the feeling I thought I'd get from Tatum when moving but never did. It's nice to finally feel appreciated.

"You did all this?" I ask, looking at Lou.

She nods with a smile. "We've all missed you." And boy have I missed them.

Everyone tugs on our arms, hugging and bombarding us with questions about the life we all thought I'd be living. The room is filled with loud chatter and laughter. *People are happy.*

Then there's my mom, sitting alone, in silence. Her eyes bounce from person to person, knitting her eyebrows together and wandering to a place only she can go to. She's lost weight since I saw her last. Her eyes have sunken in, only slightly, but

Dear Tatum

enough for me to notice.

Our eyes meet and her shoulders relax. My name whispers from her mouth and a smile appears across her face. But it doesn't last for long. People walk over to her one by one, but it's hard for her to hold a conversation. Hosting parties used to be one of her favorite things to do. Now it's nothing but a mere inconvenience.

Finding Carson in a sea of people isn't easy. I'm not looking to chat, but to see how she looks, to see if she's okay. Boasting about how beautiful Malibu is, all while hiding the truth of what's really been going on is heavier than I thought it would be.

Shuffling through the faces, I notice hers is missing. But I might know where to find her. "Do you miss it here?" I ask. Carson stands in the doorway of her old room, leaning against the doorframe. Most of her things are still here, just in a pile in the middle of the floor.

She shrugs. "I can live without it," she finally says.

But I'm not sure she can.

I'm not sure I can, either.

"Please come home," Tatum begs. His eyes are broken with glass breaking tears. It's hard to tell if they're phony or legit. I'd say they're probably somewhere right in the middle. "Please tell me you're coming home." I wish the word home felt more like home. But Malibu doesn't feel like anything to me.

"I'm coming back," I say. "So stop asking."

"Things will be different. No Sadie. No Alisa. No secrets. Just us." *Just us.*

Getting rid of Tatum and throwing everything we've had out the window doesn't feel right. It's not that easy. We're all fucked up in our own way, but that doesn't mean I go back and pretend nothing happened.

He's been trying to convince me our lives will somehow be normal by the time I get back. That somehow Sadie will have moved almost all of her things out of the house. I'll be able to move in with him. And Alisa has already been 'let go'.

He's convincing me all of his baggage has dried up.

He's taken care of all of it.

In a matter of a week—

Gone.

Impressive. Telling. But bullshit.

"Harper!" I hear my mom screaming. I hang up on Tatum and tremble down the stairs. I find her on the ground, next to her bed. Breath quick, eyebrows narrowed, shoulders slouched, hand bruised.

The words *I'm so sorry* play on repeat. Her voice, so broken, shatters my heart. Her eyes are dull and full of sorrow. She looks...*broken*. "I don't know how I got here," she cries.

The lamp's been knocked to the ground. Her curtain is ripped. She's been here for a while. Her old age is showing, again. Her bones, so weak, wouldn't allow her to get up on her own.

Heavy footsteps slam down each step. It's both Carson and Lou rushing down the stairs. "Is everything okay?" Lou asks while Carson's mouth gapes open. Her face turns pale, too pale like she's ready to faint.

Carson stands further back than Lou, but that's her thing. She fears getting too close; close enough that if something were to happen, she'd feel it. Feel the disruption weaving in and out of her. She's always been this way, but today is the day I understand it. I understand a part of her because this hurts. *Bad*. Really, really bad.

"Grammy, what happened?" Lou's voice snaps me back into the moment.

I'm sorry is still all she can get out.

"It's okay, Mom," I tell her. "Don't apologize."

The waiting room is packed, per usual. People are pacing back and forth, coughing with their mouths open and whining to their company about how sick they are. Oh, and we can't forget about the people who only open their mouths to complain about how

Dear Tatum

long they've been waiting.

But despite the annoyance, I'm thankful. Thankful their discrepancies can yank me away from the thoughts pulling on my soul. Broken bones. Distant mind. Thoughts unclear. *Reasons unknown.* I can't imagine the thoughts raging through my mother's mind. Did she understand what was happening? Will she ever remember how she ended up on the floor to begin with? *Will her memory continue to fall apart?*

These thoughts pull on me with no regret. But I do regret thinking of all the things we never got to say to one another. How we both failed each other. It's hard not to think about how things could have been different for us. How each move I've made in my life could have affected our relationship. Would she have gone out of her way to try to understand me if my father wasn't so harsh? Would we have been friends? Would she have been more of a mother to me?

I don't know the answers. But if I were to ask, she wouldn't know either. I think that's what hurts the most. I waited too long. *Too, too long.*

THIRTY-NINE

Harper

Carson and Lou both continue to ask when my mom is coming home. And every time I lie. "Hopefully in a couple of days." I smile to try to wash away the truth. But you can't wash away what's here to stay.

Grandma isn't coming home. How do you say that to your kids? Saying it out loud creates a throbbing pain I can't get under control. One I can't stomach.

I stand in the doorway of her room, my head leaning on the frame. It's hard to escape the memories floating around my mind when they're playing out in front of me.

Her smile dances through my head. It makes me smile. She's young again, fresh-faced with no wrinkles and hair perfectly done, with possibly too much hairspray.

I don't know how much time I have left to create more memories with her. But I'm not sure if I want more. I'm afraid of what she'll leave me with. Wanting more? Wishing for something different? Wanting a reality that wasn't meant for us? I don't want to do that to myself. Nor do I want to do it to her.

"She's not coming home is she?" I look over and see Carson standing next to me. Our eyes don't meet. It's another one of her *things.*

"No," I say. "She's not." I don't bother looking at her. Her sniffles give away her thoughts. "It's the best place for her." My stomach hollows as I try not only to convince Carson but also myself.

"I hope so," she sighs.

I hope so, too.

Lou still has no idea my mom isn't coming home. The words still won't escape my mouth. And not telling her the truth opens my eyes to things I couldn't see before.

Things like lying. It's silly, I know. But isn't it strange? As human beings, it's in our nature to reject any and all lies, along with un-honest people. Which makes sense as to why we feel less than whenever we find ourselves in a situation to tell a lie.

But why do we lie? We all think we're worthy of the truth, but what if we aren't looking at it the right way? You see, it's not that I've decided not to tell Lou about my mom being in a nursing home because I believe she's unworthy of knowing, but because I know how much this decision hurts and will hurt for all of us.

Truth causes pain. I've always known this, but I never really understood it until now. Knowing is not understanding. Understanding is a gift that forces you to see from a different perspective. And I'm forced to look at this from a different perspective.

She's safe.

Maybe this is why Tatum lies. Maybe he's scared. Maybe letting me in terrifies him to the point of exhaustion. But either way, there's truth to be told.

What do I want? What am I sacrificing being with him? *Is it worth it?* Being honest with myself first can only bring me what I've been missing.

It's disappointing I've waited this long to be honest with myself. Living in such a dour world, I hadn't realized my own happiness was something that was missing. Without the coin of honesty, your world becomes a never-ending web of disasters. And it's a vicious cycle that'll never end if you choose to ignore it.

For the first time in my life, I feel in control. I understand what I need as a woman. But I've come to realize the most difficult part will be confronting Tatum about my own desires and allowing him to come to his own decision on whether or not he can fulfill that.

Telling him will mean keeping myself accountable, and having the strength to walk away if he can't provide me with what I need. And of course, vice versa. *What if I can't provide him with what he needs?* Then I'll have to walk away. It's tragic when realizing you and the person you love aren't capable of giving happiness to each other. But if you're not happy, what are you?

You're nothing.

Brandy: I heard ur home.
Me: let me guess. adam told u?
Brandy:

The typing bubble pops up and down, but she never responds. Of course, Adam told her. Who else would?

Brandy: come outside.

I peek out my window to see Brandy leaning against her car door. "You must be kidding me," I say to myself. "What are you doing here?"

"Just let me explain," she says. "Why do you think we lost contact? You think I just forgot about you and everything we've been through together?"

I shrug.

"You're a sister to me. I'd do literally anything to protect you."

"Fucking my brother is protecting me?" I shake my head. "Yeah, real protective. I feel so safe now, Brandy, thank you. And thanks to your boyfriend for spilling what I keep hidden. Real classy."

"He's not my boyfriend," she says, clenching her jaw together.

"Like that makes it any better."

"Adam hates that you're gay." She says it as if I haven't lived every inch of that hatred. "But it's not what you think."

"Enlighten me," I laugh.

"He knows what comes with being gay. He knows the judgment and the hate. He never wanted that for you." She stops for a moment and I'm afraid of what she needs to say next. "He wanted to..."

"Scare me straight?" She nods, bowing her head. "Hate to break it to the both of you, but that's not how it works."

"I know," she says. "And he told me about your dad and what he did to you. It's horrible, Harper. And it made me angry that even until this day, you've never trusted me enough to tell me."

"Do you think that's something I want to tell people?"

"Adam was angry at your dad," she says. "He didn't know any other way to react than to lash out and hurt you, too."

"And you think that's okay?"

"Of course not," she says. "But we made a deal, Harper."

"Which was?"

"You're really going to make me say it?"

I nod. *Of course, I am.*

She takes in a much-needed breath before admitting the reason she's gone so far behind my back. "As long as I slept with him, he wouldn't tell anyone else."

Betrayal has engraved itself onto her skin, screaming too loud for me to ignore. It's too loud for her to ignore. She understands the root of my anger.

But, as much as I hate her for it, she did something no one else would. She chose me over her own feelings. It's kind of hard to stay mad at that. I guess she really was just trying to protect me.

FORTY

Harper

The front door opens and I almost bolt up the stairs, but Adam's in front of me, blocking my only way out. "Hey," he says.

"Looking forward to the court date?" I ask, trying to brush by him, but he blocks me, *again*.

"I actually wanted to talk to you about that." His voice is soft. His temper isn't high. It almost feels like he's...sad. "I dropped the case."

My eyes bolt to his, but he's not looking at me. "Why?"

"Because, Harper, this isn't how we should be living."

"Are you okay?" I ask, wondering what's gotten into him. He's being way too nice.

"I know you know about me and Brandy. I know what she told you." He wipes his lips with his hand, almost as if he's wiping away the words coming off of them. "I've been doing a lot of thinking while you've been away. Why didn't you tell me you were seeing a man? Isn't that what you thought I wanted?"

"Why would I? So you can get off on changing me? Adam, I'm still the same person. *I'm still gay.*" He bows his head as if he's disappointed. "Did you think I was straight now? Is that why you dropped the case? Is that why you're being nice?" I start to raise my voice but stops before it gets too loud.

"No!" He yells. "I'm sorry, Harper. I wanted to be like Dad when I was growing up. And before I knew…" He stops. He doesn't want to say it out loud. And I'm glad because I don't want to hear it. "I was too young to understand any of it. And then when I heard Mom and Dad yelling at you about kissing a girl, I just…"

"You just what, Adam?"

"I just believed everything they said. Did everything they did. I hated you for it. I hated that you would put your own beliefs in front of taking care of yourself. I hated that Mom and Dad spent more time disciplining you than taking care of me. I used to look up to Dad. I wanted to be just like him. And I was so angry at the world for all its stupid standards. For all the judgment. *All of it.* The world is a cruel fucking place, Harper. I didn't want that for you."

I look away from him as my eyes start to fill with tears that feel like they're ripping apart who I am. I want to believe him. I want to have a brother who loves me. For me. For exactly who I am.

"I know sorry won't cut it. And I know I've pushed you away. But I am sorry, Harper. I really am."

I hope he is sorry. But I also hope one day we can be friends, and we can sit down and have a drink together. I hope one day we can laugh together. And I hope one day he can be…*my brother.*

Nothing Adam says will ever take back for what he did, but I'll take it for what it is now because this is somehow a start to a relationship I never thought I'd have. And this time, I don't want to wait too long.

FORTY-ONE
Harper

His eyes, so tender and shrill, swaddle me into a suffocating cocoon. And though his eyes mimic a clear blue sky, I can see a storm brewing in the distance. There's a smile sitting on his face, but it's more for appearance than anything else.

"I'm happy you're home," he says. His body trembles in his seat as if it's impossible for him to keep still. Digging at me, he looks for a response, but when it doesn't come he starts to teeter.

I readjust in my seat, sitting back, keeping my hands on my lap. Getting too close will give him an opportunity to reel me back in. "We need to have a serious conversation, Tatum." He nods. "What were you thinking?" Still, he says nothing. It's like he's scared of hearing his own voice. "I'm afraid this isn't for us," I finally say.

He stutters trying to explain what's been happening. Excusing his behavior by claiming it as *miscommunication*. "This is just a rough patch," he says, voice cracking mid-sentence. He tries to clear his throat but it's still as jarring as it was before. "My divorce will be final soon. Everything will be better for us."

"Your divorce will be final because Sadie's done with you, Tatum. Not because you're done with her."

Dear Tatum

He tries to explain and deny. He tries to manipulate me into thinking Sadie and Alisa were coaxing me into a game to force him and I apart. But the proof is in front of me. The more I lean on what I know, I'm pushed further away from him. Tatum can't give me what I need. And I don't have to ask to know.

"Where were you when you said you were working on the convention?"

"Alisa made that up, Harper. I didn't lie about it." He bites his lip and lowers his stare.

"Where were you, Tatum?"

He throws his head in his hands and sits there for a minute. I wonder what he's thinking. I wonder if he's contemplating telling the truth—*for once*. And I hope he does. Not only do I deserve the truth, but he deserves to be honest with himself. He deserves to be set free, too.

"I was with Wren."

My heart drops. *Wren?*

"I haven't been completely honest with you," he says. I get Sadie. I kind of get Alisa. But Wren? I thought that was over. "Remember the night we graduated? The party?" I nod, remembering that night like it was yesterday. "I wanted to leave early because I knew if I got home too late my mom would be pissed and I was tired," he says. "I went looking for Wren and when I found her—" His voice starts to fade. "The two of you were kissing."

What. The. Fuck.

"Harper," he says. "I was so mad. And I was mad at you for trying to steal Wren away from me. It was like you thought she'd be better yours than mine."

"What are you saying right now?"

He ignores me and continues to talk. "I confronted her. She begged me not to tell anyone. She said her mom would disown her and she was embarrassed by what happened. It was my out. After everything she held over my head, I finally had something."

This is sick, right? My boyfriend is confessing to me the reason him and his ex broke up was because of me.

I'm the one that broke them up.

I'm the one *she* kissed.

The one he told me about.

And I don't know what to say because it's beyond what the truth holds.

"The night of the reunion, I saw you, and all of the emotions flooded back. I was angry and hurt you tried to do that to me. I wanted to get back at you for trying to hurt me." His voice softens like what he's about to say will excuse what he's done. "But in the midst of everything, I realized that you aren't that person anymore. You're someone I can actually see myself with. I fell in love with you, Harper." All of this because of *one* night of hurt. *Wow.*

He used me to get back at me. *To hurt me.* He did all of this on purpose. He did all of this because of one kiss.

He bores his eyes into mine trying to find the response he wants. The corners of his lips smirk to cover up the truth of his intentions. He's desperate to be innocent.

But clarity comes with his confession. This was never meant for us. He was never meant for me. My chest is on fire, burning from the heat pouring off of him. For the first time, I can see through his mask. I can see who he is.

A damaged soul.

He's survived this long by only looking out for himself. Since he was young he's had to do things the wrong way to survive. Maybe he's lost himself. Maybe he needs help.

Maybe.

But I can't be the one to help him. I can't give him what he needs. I can't be the one to hurt in order to help him survive.

I need to live.

I need to survive.

I need to be who I'm supposed to be.

I push out of my chair and stand up. He stares at me confused. He tries to force words out of his mouth, but he's stuttering and not making any sense.

He's following me to my car, but still, I refuse to speak. He's

Dear Tatum

non-deserving of my breath. I turn around and look at him one last time. He doesn't stand as tall. His shoulders aren't as strong as I thought they were and his eyes don't make me melt.

And out of nowhere, I throw my coffee at him. *Oh my god.* I laugh with my hand over my mouth. I can't believe I just did that. Do I regret it? Not at all. Out of all the things he's done to me, to Sadie, to Alisa...he deserves a little coffee on his shirt.

"Good-bye, Tatum."

FORTY-TWO
Harper

The waves crash against the rocks in front of the house. I listen closely to see if I can hear any of its pain being let go. Somehow, it helps me relax. It helps me breathe. It helps me find comfort. And it reminds me that I'm okay.

Carson and I are moving back home in a week. Worrying about the judgment of others isn't something I've found worrying me lately. I'm letting go for the first time.

Brandy promised to stop sleeping with Adam in exchange for keeping my secret quiet. If he's going to tell, then he's going to tell. I'm not a product of what my father did to me. I'm not a victim anymore.

Carson walks onto the balcony, and without words or an explanation, she reaches her arms out and pulls me towards her. I don't question it. I squeeze her tighter. I don't think we've ever hugged. At least not since she was a kid. It makes me feel more of a mother. Like somehow she needs this.

Like somehow...*she needs me.*

She pulls away and looks at me, eyes wide, and filled with confidence. "I finished my book," she says.

"Are you kidding me?" I pull her back and hold her again,

but this time she pulls away.

"About two years ago," she says, pausing. "Today, I got a publisher." My jaw drops to the floor. *Holy shit.*

"I didn't even—"

"It's okay," she says. "I didn't really want to make it a big deal until it was official. Thought I'd spare myself the embarrassment if I failed." I press my lips together, ashamed I've allowed my daughter to feel so isolated—that even her biggest accomplishment needs to be kept hidden, even from me.

Today I feel like Carson and I began again. Like somewhere down the road her and I will actually be friends. And even though it'll take time, I'm okay with waiting. I'm okay with putting in the work.

If there's one thing I learned about moving down here, it's that this move was never about Tatum, or us, or the life I thought we'd share. It was about finding who I am as a person. It was about finding my strength, my heart, and who I *need* to be.

Time fleets and most of the time we don't even realize it. We spend so much time on the things that hurt us, we forget to appreciate what makes us.

Sometimes we drive on a path that isn't meant for us, promising ourselves things that won't fit in our life. But sometimes being on the wrong path can bring you exactly where you need to be. Because along the way you find pieces of yourself you lost so long ago. You find what really matters. And if you're lucky enough, you too find yourself, again.

EMILY REILLY

Dear Tatum,

I don't know where to start this letter, but I won't sit here and bash who you are. We know who you are. We've seen it. Thinking about what we've gone through, I've realized we were never in love. We were connected by the pain we share. It's what kept me coming back to you. I was comfortable knowing I could wallow with someone who has drowned as much as I have. But Tatum, there is light to be shed. There is a truth you need to know. The night of graduation, I didn't kiss Wren. She kissed me. Wren didn't hate me in high school because I was gay. She hated me because she was. Her mom walked in on us on the last day of eighth grade. It was our first kiss. She took control of Wren that day and forced her to be someone she wasn't, just like my father tried to do with me. I'm not saying this to take from what the two of you had, but to be honest, because honesty is something we both lack. Being gay in a religious home was torture. But truthfully, I think it had less to do with religion and more to do with how horrible of a person my father was. He tried to change me. He used his hands to maneuver what I liked. He thought experience with a man would change me. He didn't make me want men. He made me want to stay away from them. But then, I found you and everything changed. I thought, maybe I wasn't gay. Maybe I just never found the right person. And when you kissed me... it changed me. I saw something in you and I clung to it. So afraid of being alone, I

224

Dear Tatum

needed to have you. I was tired of being lonely. I was tired of being sad. But being with you didn't change any of that. Actually, I was sadder being with you. I was lonelier. But I learned a lot about myself being with you. I learned that my happiness starts and ends with me. I don't need you or anyone else to give that to me. I hope one day you can free yourself from your own dark past. No one deserves to be lonely. No one deserves to be stuck. It took me fifty years to figure it out, but I'm glad I finally did. You helped me with that, so thank you. But as for us, I think it's better if we go our separate ways. There's nothing connecting us anymore. Not even our pain.

Take care Tatum,
Harper

FORTY-THREE

Sadie

It's been six months without Tatum. I've had six months of growing and learning, and I already feel somewhat lighter. I still have a lot of healing ahead, but the shadows that once lurked in my corner, seem to be falling behind.

Tatum stops by to see the kids every once in a while, but I think most of it is to try and nudge his way back into my life. But I've learned to disconnect from the words he spews. Tatum isn't going to change and I'm okay with that now because it's not for me to understand anymore.

As for August, I've neither seen nor tried to talk to him. I've gone as far as switching coffee shops so we don't run into each other. I'm not sure if he's still seeing that girl, but if he is I hope she makes him happy. It's the least he deserves.

Walking up to the counter at White Sugar, I order my normal coffee. The barista is smiling. She glows with an innocence I find missing in most people. I smile back and hope she never loses sight of her own freedom. Because when you're not looking for it, it's easy to lose.

Sitting down, I pull out the folder for the new business I'm starting. This is something I should've done a long time ago, but never did. Time got away from me. *I got away from me.* And if I don't make something of myself now, then I won't just be letting myself down, but also my kids. I need to show them that it's okay to take risks if the end result is something you really want.

A shadow appears in the corner of my eye, but I don't look up immediately. I assume it's someone trying to get to another table, but when their hand reaches out for a chair, I look up.

What in the world?

"Can I sit?" I bite my lip while nodding yes at the same time.

"What are you doing here?" I ask.

"I came looking for you," he says. "It wasn't hard. I mean, this is the second-best coffee shop in town." We both laugh. But he's right, it is, but I still miss The Coffee Bean.

Every wisp of air is blown from my lungs, leaving me without any air to breathe. "I thought—" He shakes his head interrupting my thought.

"She wasn't what I was looking for." August's eyes stare at me from across the table, pulling me into him. Butterflies dance around my stomach for the first time in so long. I press my palms together and lift my hands to my lips, covering my smile. "I'm sorry for letting you walk away that night," he says. But he has nothing to be sorry for, *especially that*. I needed this time to be alone. Somehow, it's brought me back to life.

I've festered on my faults. I've thought of ways to expose them without hurting too many people. But I've realized there won't ever be a perfect time or way to let this out. And if I want to be with August, I need to come clean now. There's no time left to waste. And if he changes his mind about being with me, then he changes his mind. I can't change what I've done, and I don't want to try to change how he feels.

He grabs my hand and brings it to his lips. "I need to tell you something." My voice shakes as I try to get the words out.

His thoughts comb through his mind, going over every possibility of what it is I need to confess. I want to turn around and run. My stomach churns, but it vomits up exactly what it is August needs to know.

Every secret and every piece of pain I've been keeping to

myself, I say out loud. I don't look at August. I'm scared of what he looks like. I'm scared of what he's thinking. Fifteen years worth of pain, gone, flying in the open for anyone to know. It almost feels good. *Almost.*

August takes a deep breath before placing his finger under my chin. He lifts my head, "I'm so sorry you've kept this in." His eyes show no trace of anger. As a matter of fact, they almost look happy. "It's going to take some time to get used to," he says. "But I'm not letting you go, Sadie. You've been gone for far too long."

I don't swallow the knot in my throat. I allow it to surface with the tears it brings. I cry. August cries. We have no shame feeling our feelings in the middle of White Sugar. We even start to laugh realizing how silly we probably look to the people here. But neither of us cares.

Our red string connects. No matter where we go, no matter how far we stray, we'll always find our way back to one another. Our red string will always be our way back.

Always.

Dear Tatum

Dear Tatum,

I'm not sure how to dive into this letter. I have a lot to say and a lot to admit. The past fifteen years have been a whirlwind of emotions for each of us. There are things I've kept hidden away, things I'm ashamed of, and things I wish I handled differently. Our marriage wasn't entirely based on love and I assume that's accurate on your end too. I want you to know, I loved you for a long time. Though I feel it wasn't for the right reasons, love was still present, which is why I stayed for as long as I did. You meant a lot to me, more than I can express. We both know we started a relationship in a vile way and it hurt a lot of people we cared about. But what you don't know and what I failed to be honest about is that our affair didn't start out of spite for August. In fact, it started because of how much I love him. There are things you still don't know about me, things I didn't think I'd ever share. I was sick, Tatum. I had a disease I thought would kill me. I was confused about what was happening to my body. I faced it alone as a young adult and again when we met. I didn't tell anyone, not even August, my own husband who vowed to be there for me in sickness and in health. I wasn't afraid of telling him because I thought he would leave, I was afraid because I knew he wouldn't. I knew he would have stuck by my side every step of the way. He would've closed his practice before leaving me alone to face any doctor's appointment I had. The last thing I ever wanted was to leave him in mourning. I dreamt a lot about the life he would live without me. It was painful to watch and think about. It consumed me. I thought long and hard about what I would do. Do I tell him or do I leave him? I couldn't get the words out. And I couldn't leave on my own. So I did what I thought I had to do. I needed him to leave me. I needed him to hate me. I hurt him on purpose. It was single handedly the most painful thing I ever had to do. I thought that would keep him away. As painful as it felt at the time, I thought I'd never see his face again. I was content being married to you. I fell for you in the midst of the most chaotic time of my life. When I felt vulnerable and small, you were there without even realizing how much you were helping. But August didn't stay away for long. A couple of years after you and I were married, we were blessed with our

Dear Tatum

first baby boy. I knew you had somewhat of a hard time accepting we'd be parents. You didn't think you were ready, maybe quite possibly thought you weren't meant to be a father. But nine months later you were staring into a small face that looked just like me and nothing like you. You accepted that you were a father and you were finally happy about it. I couldn't take that away from you. It's selfish, I know, but I knew why he didn't look like you. It pains me. It's kept me with you for all these years. It's the reason I've excused your actions. You were happy looking at him. You even made a joke about how he gets his looks from me. I cringed at the thought that maybe you'd see a little of August in him too. I was never prepared to tell you this. I was never prepared to admit what I had done. A lie like this is unforgivable and I understand that. I understand this lie hurts more than one person. It hurts a line of people. It's crushed me since he was born. I've allowed it to consume me into the shadows that live behind us. But what I've finally realized is that no matter how many times I forgive you or whether or not you'd ever stop cheating on me, I'll never be happy. I'd be stuck, lost, in these cryptic shadows forever. I

EMILY REILLY

want to find my way out. I know my faults have to be aired out for that to happen, so I'm setting them free from the cage they've been locked in. This is not easy to say and I know it's not easy to hear. There is nothing I can say to excuse my actions and quite frankly, I'm not here to excuse them. I won't say I'm sorry because I told you before, sometimes sorry doesn't cut it, and I know that's the case for this. I don't expect forgiveness. I'll take whatever you hand me, whether it's a legal action or nothing but an hour long screaming match. But I won't sit around anymore and let my past affect my future. Despite my wrongs, I deserve some happiness. I deserve love, real love. I'm not sure we ever experienced that together, but I hope one day you'll find it. I hope one day, you'll find someone who makes you so happy you don't feel like you need to cheat. Maybe you will or maybe no woman will satisfy you completely, but I'll pray for you, Tatum. I'll pray you find some happiness of your own. I pray you'll be set free from your own demons. Thank you for these years. Thank you for the countless lessons you've taught me. I will never forget them. But it's time for me to move on. It's time for me to for-

Dear Tatum

give myself and allow myself what I deserve. No more sitting in the dark. No more sitting in the shadows. I'm letting this go. I'm letting you go and I'm setting myself free.

Goodbye Tatum,
Sadie

Tatum

Pain overpowers love
Pain overpowers me
I muted my own strength
And pained the people that loved me.

I'm left alone
Cold and broken, in a lonely world
I ripped my life apart
To be a man I'm not at heart.

I pray for the day
All the heartache fades away
I'm sorry for what I've done
Now you can finally say, *you've won*.

About the Author

Emily Reilly is best known for her writing. She is the author of *Saving Ivy* and was a guest speaker at Africa's largest writing event, *BOOKICON*. It's easy to say that her true calling is creating work that people are able to connect with. Emily loves meeting and talking to her readers! You can find her Instagram, *@emreilly*, to keep up with all her latest news and upcoming releases.

COMING NEXT

Always Loved You

"What happens when you experience the essence of true love? Where do you go from there? Do you run from it? Or do you run towards it? Love isn't an easy road. It rocks from side to side. It goes to places you don't want to visit. But yet... that's all we strive for. We live for it. At least I know I do. Love is the only thing this world has to offer that never dulls. Everyone's definition is different, but I'd like to think each one means the same thing. Always Loved You is one of the many stories love brings us. I'm excited for this journey and to share another piece of me with all of you." – Em Reilly